OMINOUS WORLD

Emily Regan

Created by E.S. Fortune

ISBN: 978-0-9987732-4-7

Cover design by Katie McLeod
Title page image used under Creative Commons License CC0,
the contents of which can be found here:
https://creativecommons.org/publicdomain/zero/1.0/legalcode

First Edition

OMINOUS WORLD

Emily Regan

Created by E.S. Fortune

1

SCARLETT FELT THE sun before she saw it, a slow burn on her skin. She blinked away the red heat behind her closed eyelids and squinted in the bright yellow bath of sunlight. Scarlett looked down at the ground for a moment, shielding her eyes to let them adjust. Her shadow was almost directly beneath her, hardly stretching out at all. She pushed herself up into a sitting position and felt the grit of the dirt beneath her. Scarlett looked down at her naked body, slowly growing rosy in the sun. She couldn't imagine that she'd removed her own clothes and headed into the desert, apparently alone, but she had no idea who could have done this. Actually, that wasn't entirely true; she could imagine a lot of someones who could and would have done this. Being a mercenary wasn't exactly the best way to make friends.

Scarlett glanced around in an attempt to get her bearings, but there wasn't much to see. Beside her was a dying tree, its trunk brown and dry and broken, and a large rock. In the distance, she saw a plateaued mountain range, and off to one side, she thought she could make out some hills. The landscape between was dotted with the occasional scrub bush and small rocks, but was otherwise vacant. Except for her, of course. Scarlett knew better than to assume an empty landscape was truly empty, but, for the moment, her sharp gaze couldn't find another soul. She closed her eyes for a moment, the heat baking down on her like an oven. Scarlett knew she needed to get out of the sun, but her head felt so watery and unclear. She felt a small tickle on her foot and opened her eyes, expecting to see an errant piece of scrub grass or a trickle of sweat. Instead, she saw a large black scorpion, its body shiny in the noon sun. It's stinger was poised threateningly over its head, ready to drop at a moment's notice like the needle of a sewing machine. Scarlett instinctively kicked out her foot, finding a strength reserve she hadn't known she possessed at that moment, and pushed herself backwards until her back hit the large rock. She watched the scorpion sail away, its descent a smooth arc, until it dropped out of sight far enough away to where she couldn't see it any longer. She breathed deeply, her heart racing at the momentary burst of adrenaline, and she let her hands drop to the dirt on either side of her. That was when her left hand hit the canteen. Scarlett grabbed the warm plastic container and immediately felt the weight of the water sloshing within it. She quickly unscrewed the top, her mouth and throat growing almost unbearably dry in these final seconds before feeling the relief of the liquid. As she gulped the water, the rational voice in the back of Scarlett's brain reminded her that chugging so much water while dehydrated could make her vomit, thereby defeating the purpose. However, her physical self drowned out her mind and told it where it could stick practicalities like "logic." The water was warm from sitting in the sun, but Scarlett didn't mind as the liquid poured over her dry tongue. When she'd drained the canteen, she immediately felt sick. God, why had she done that?

I told you so, a small voice in the back of her mind said. Scarlett would have told the voice to shut up if she weren't focusing all of her strength on keeping the water down in her stomach. She evened her breath, slowly pulling in air through her nose before slowly expelling it between pursed lips. *Good air in, 2, 3, 4, bad air out, 2, 3, 4.* After a minute or so, the nausea subsided and Scarlett felt fairly certain that the water would stay down. She relaxed against the rock again as she cradled the empty plastic canteen against her chest before glancing around to see if whoever had left her there had given her anything else. If they'd gone to the effort of removing all of her clothing, she knew it wasn't likely they'd left her a fresh set of clothes or anything with which to cover herself, but perhaps they'd left her other provisions. Maybe a second canteen, or food. Scarlett also knew it wasn't likely they'd left her a weapon of some kind. They'd stripped her of the simple defense of clothing—a knife or a gun was clearly out of the question. At first, she didn't see anything else around her, save for gritty dirt and small rocks. But then, pinned underneath a larger stone, Scarlett saw the corner of a piece of dirty paper. She leaned over and gently tugged the paper free, careful not to rip it, and read the note written in a very familiar hand.

Sorry, Scarlett, no hard feelings.
It's just business.

Realization and anger surged through Scarlett, temporarily making her forget her exhaustion and the heat. She grabbed the empty canteen and hurled it away. It bounced twice, before it lay motionless, gone the way of the scorpion.

"God dammit, Mel," Scarlett muttered.

2

SCARLETT PUSHED HERSELF up to her feet, using the big rock to steady herself. Her legs still felt a little weak but she knew she had to push through and keep moving. She wasn't sure where she was, but she knew she wouldn't make it for long if she stayed exposed like she was. Natural elements notwithstanding, God only knew what kind of people were in these parts. And these days, there weren't a whole lot of nice people. Evidently, even those you trusted could turn out to be not so nice either.

Scarlett's head still didn't feel quite right, but it was getting easier to focus. She used her hand to shield her eyes as she stared out across the landscape. About a mile away, near the mountain range, she saw a sign hanging between two posts. When a warm breeze blew through a moment later, Scarlett thought she saw the sign move a little in the wind. A cloth sign. Excellent. She'd have to get creative when it came to securing it, but some fabric wrapped around her would be better than no clothing at all. Certainly so when it came to the sunburn stinging her skin.

Just then, she heard the rumble of an engine, an angry buzz from far away. She instinctively hopped over the rock and hit the ground on the other side, the dirt almost hot against her skin. She was suddenly glad for the noonday sun that kept her shadow contained underneath her, rather than letting it splay out from behind the rock, giving away her position. Scarlett knew that sound could travel far across an empty landscape like a desert, so she wasn't sure how far away the noise really was. She peeked around the side of the rock by the dead tree. In the distance, she could see a black truck approaching, its tires spitting dust and rocks in its wake. Standing in the bed of the pickup was what looked like a woman with a gun, her hair pulled back out of her face. She seemed to be struggling to hang on and didn't appear to wear much clothing. All Scarlett could see was a black vest, but Scarlett wasn't about to just sit there and analyze the woman's outfit. As the truck drew closer, Scarlett ducked back around to the other side of the rock, frantically looking around for some kind of weapon. There wasn't even so much as a decent sized rock on that side. If forced, Scarlett would have to resort to hand to hand combat—but even then, there was only so much a fist could do against a gun.

The engine grew louder as a truck drew closer and Scarlett stayed put, trying to keep her breath even. *Good air in, bad air out.* Scarlett heard the brakes of the truck squeal a little, a small shriek as the vehicle came to a stop.

"What is it?" a male voice called. How many of them were there? Scarlett hadn't been able to get a look at the cab of the truck, but she figured there were two people in there, maybe three.

"Nothing," a female voice called back. "I thought I saw something, but I think it was just the tree."

"You need to get your fuckin' eyes checked," the male voice said as the truck grumbled away, leaving Scarlett once more in the quiet of the desert. She exhaled, realizing for the first time that she'd been holding her breath. She waited several more minutes, counting off the seconds with her fingertips in the dirt, before allowing herself to peek around the rock again. There was no sign of the truck anywhere, so she stood up, scanning the landscape once more.

Nobody here but us naked chickens Scarlett thought. If she was going to make it to the sign, she'd have to be quick. A truck with a gunner in the back wasn't much of a welcome wagon.

Scarlett began walking towards the sign. Her feet had some mild calluses built up on the soles, but not enough for this landscape, and small rocks and sticks stung the bottoms of her feet with nearly every step. Sweat beaded on the back of her neck and under her breasts and began to slide down her body, providing tiny rivulets of relief from the heat whenever the breeze blew by. Scarlett wanted to pull her long brown hair over one shoulder to relieve some of the heat on her neck, but she knew her hair was providing at least a little cover from the sun to her upper back, so she left it alone.

The sign was closer now and Scarlett could see the word "Coahuila" painted on it with a couple brightly colored feathers in red and yellow hanging off the sides. Coahuila—why was that word familiar? Scarlett tried to recall, but the memory was just out of reach. Her head still felt off, foggy from whatever drugs she'd been given and the heat of the sun. Scarlett figured that it was probably the name of the area, but it frustrated her that she couldn't remember why that was significant. She didn't want to cause any trouble with whomever posted the sign, but she needed to cover herself with something and the rocks and scrub brush weren't of much use to her.

Sorry, feather people Scarlett thought when she was about 10 yards from the sign. *No hard feelings. It's just fabric.*

She thought of the note and shook her head in disgust. Maybe it wasn't what she thought and Mel hadn't done this willingly. Maybe she had been forced to write that note. But by whom? Scarlett wasn't sure yet. She wished she could remember what happened. The last thing she could recall was sitting with Mel and the team in the tavern after the last run. Scarlett had been drinking, they all had, but then . . . she didn't know what came next. Somehow she'd gone from a tavern in Virginia to a desert that she knew couldn't geographically be anywhere near Virginia. How long had she been out? It had to have been days. But how many? Scarlett hated the idea of losing time like that. She looked down at her body. She looked a little thinner than she remembered, but not alarmingly so. She figured she couldn't have been out for more than a couple days, three at the most. The thought of food made her stomach grumble. The first order of business was to try and keep herself from dying of exposure in the desert, but the second definitely needed to be finding food. She almost regretted kicking away the scorpion. It wouldn't have been an ideal snack, but some food is better than no food. Her stomach grumbled again and Scarlett put a hand on her belly to quiet it. The feeling stopped, but the noise did not. It took her a moment to realize that the rumbling she heard wasn't her stomach, but an engine. She turned around and saw the black truck barreling towards her, the gunner's rifle pointed straight at her.

Scarlett gave one last look up at the sign and, with a frustrated groan, started sprinting towards the rock face of the mountains. Her feet protested painfully with each step on a jagged rock, but she pushed forward, knowing that a bullet would be far more painful than anything the desert floor was going to dish up at her. Behind her, she heard the truck screech to a stop but she didn't turn around. Turning around could get her a bullet in the head. Her decision to keep looking forward was confirmed when she heard the crack of a rifle and a bullet splintered the rock face up ahead.

"Stop, you fucking cunt!" a man's voice yelled. "Stop shooting!"

Another bullet went off, exploding a puff of dust on the ground somewhere off to Scarlett's right.

"Stop!" There were two voices now, two angry men screaming. Scarlett heard truck doors slam shut but she didn't turn around, she just keep pushing forward. *A moving target is harder to hit* she coached herself as she ran. The blood thrummed in her ears as she ran and Scarlett had no idea if the people in the truck were chasing her or not. The only thing she knew for sure was that she couldn't stop running if she wanted to have a chance of keeping her head intact. Up ahead, there was a break in the rock face, a narrow path that Scarlett thought she could fit through. At this point, it was her only hope. She ran up to the opening and jumped through sideways. Her back scraped the wall but she made it. The path widened a little and she kept running, deftly making her way into the mountain pass.

It was then that Scarlett heard the screaming start. She didn't look back.

3

ONE OF THE Slavers, Crick, jumped into the back of the truck where the scout stood and yanked her down by her hair. She hit the truck bed hard, her head making a sickening thud against the metal. The scout cried out, but her voice was cut off when Crick grabbed her rifle and hit her in the face with the butt of her own gun. Her nose exploded in blood, splattering her face. Crick jumped down from the truck, his black boots landing heavily in the dirt, and yanked the scout out by her hair. She collapsed in a heap, the sun glittering off of her blood like sparkling rubies. *Only the best.* Crick stood over her for a moment, the sweat shining on his shaved head, and pulled a cat o' nine tails off of his belt. The scout's eyes widened in fear as Crick ran his fingers through the leather straps, the beaded ends clicking against one another. He kicked the scout until she lay face down in the dirt, her buttocks and legs exposed. Crick brought the cat o' nine tails down hard, the straps snapping against the scout's already scarred skin as the metal beads split her flesh. She screamed and her hands scratched at the dry ground, desperately searching for something to hold onto. The whip came down again and again, the sound getting wetter and wetter as her blood began to flow in earnest. The scout cried, unable to do little more than lie there as her blood arced off the whip and sprayed the dirt. The second Slaver walked around the back of the truck and kicked the scout in the side. She cried out and jerked to the side, her open wounds staining the desert ground. Kip kicked her again. Her breath shot out of her in a wheeze and she tried to draw another breath but before she could, her body curled around a third kick.

"How fucking stupid are you?" Crick yelled, stomping on her right calf.

The scout cried out, her voice weak and pitiful like the mewl of a kitten.

"It's a fucking feather!" Crick shouted, pointing at the sign. "A feather! Don't *ever* fucking fire into Eagle territory!"

Crick kicked the scout again, flipping her onto her back. The scout cried wordlessly as the dirt ground into her raw, broken flesh. Crick grinned sadistically and brought the whip down on her bare stomach. The scream caught in the scout's throat and came out as more of a strangled, choked moan. Crick spit on the red stripes across the scout's stomach, but she couldn't even feel it.

Kip straightened up, casually brushing the dirt off his black pants before straightening the black leather vest he wore over his deeply suntanned barrel chest.

"Too bad for you, this is a lesson you only learn once," Kip said, pulling an evil-looking knife from his belt. The blade shone, mirroring the sun's glare as the metal curved menacingly.

"Please," she gasped, a trickle of blood slowly falling from her split lip. Kip ignored her as he examined the knife in his hands, turning it this way and that in the dry sunshine. Crick stepped back, grinning widely, his eyes hard and lustful. He was enjoying this, excited for the show. Kip bent down and touched a finger beneath the scout's chin, lifting her face to his.

"If I were you, I'd save your breath," Kip advised. "You'll need it for when I start cutting."

The scout trembled, unable to do more than wait. Even if her gun hadn't been taken from her and had she been able to point it and pull the trigger, she wouldn't have. She was obedient, she followed orders. She did as she was told. Her loyalty held her in place as she cringed at the pain currently wracking her body and the pain that was to come. She closed her eyes.

At the sound of gunshot, the second slaver's face exploded. Blood and bone fragments and bits of gray tissue rained down on the scout's face. She opened her eyes, shocked as she stared at what Kip's head had become. Or rather, what was left of it.

"Shit!" Crick exclaimed. He dove behind the truck as another shot rang out. The scout lay where she was, too stunned to move. Her ears were ringing and everything seemed to be moving in slow motion, like she was underwater.

Have to catch her, the scout told herself. *Make it right.* She pushed herself up into a sitting position and wiped her hand across her mouth. The scout was vaguely aware of Crick pushing past her to climb into the cab of the truck. When she brought her palm back down, it was smeared with blood and tiny clumps of gray tissue. Whose blood? She wasn't sure and at that moment, it didn't matter. All that mattered was following that girl into the rock.

Another shot rang out and the truck started.

The scout stood up and reached limply for the truck but the tires kicked up a cloud of dust, stinging the eye that hadn't already swollen shut. The truck pulled away as more shots were fired, spraying her legs with small rocks. Another shot was fired and the scout heard it clang off the back of the truck. She watched dumbly as it drove away. As it receded into the distance, the scout turned and looked towards the rock face. There was the opening that woman had disappeared through. *Have to catch her. Make it right.* With great pain that made her cry out, she knelt down and grabbed the barrel of her rifle, still warm. The scout limped towards the opening in the mountain, dragging her gun behind her. It slipped out of her slick grasp, but she barely noticed. Her back and stomach were still in immense pain, like fire burning her from the inside out and the outside in, making it hard for her to stand upright. But she was moving. She pushed herself forward, staggering on uneven footsteps until she reached the mouth of the pathway. The scout braced herself against the sides as she squeezed through, trying not to put too much pressure on her bad leg. Her bloody legs and backside smeared against the rock wall and she cringed, suppressing another scream through gritted teeth, but she pushed onward. Now that she'd made it inside the rock, the scout moved more slowly, carefully picking her way around the rocky path.

Have to get her. Make it right. Have to get her. Make it right.

4

Scarlett's feet were raw and left red footprints behind her with every step. If the people in the truck were still pursuing her, she'd left them a pretty clear trail of breadcrumbs with which to find her. The screams followed her through the mountain pass until she reached a narrowing of the pathway walls, making it almost impossible for Scarlett to push through. The walls were tight and rough and Scarlett paused, feeling like a cornered rat as she examined the very narrow opening. She'd lost some weight since the tavern in Virginia, but she wasn't sure it was enough to get through. *Either get in there or go back out to face those fucking psychos* she told herself. Scarlett hesitated and then carefully wedged herself in sideways. She made it about halfway through until her body came to a complete stop. Scarlett struggled against the rock but found she couldn't move forward or backwards. *Great job, idiot.* She pushed harder, the rock digging hard into her skin. *Shit, shit, shit.* Scarlett felt the panic begin to set in and she tried to take a breath to calm herself, but she could feel her lips trembling. Fear began to swell in her like a wave as she pushed against the rock walls around her, banging her hands against the coarse surface. Her heartbeat thundered in her chest and Scarlett clawed at the walls, desperately trying to pull herself through. *I have to get out, I have to get out, have to get out, have to get out, have to—*

A shot rang out, the sound echoing down the mountain pass. The sudden blast of noise gave her a rush of adrenaline and Scarlett hurled herself through the narrowing, painfully scraping free before stumbling to her knees. The rock had clawed her skin, the soft tissues of her breasts and backside were raw and biting with pain, but she was moving forward. Scarlett wasn't totally sure what had happened back there, back by the sign, but she thought it was safe to assume the woman had been shot. As Scarlett kept moving forward, a thought occurred to her. The men hadn't been yelling at her, they'd been yelling at the scout in the truck. Why had the men told her to stop shooting? Was it possible that they weren't chasing Scarlett anymore? But if they'd stopped, was it because a greater danger lay within the mountain? Scarlett didn't know. It was hard to think clearly at the moment between her bloody feet and her dry tongue that sat thickly and uncomfortably in her mouth. She desperately hoped there would be some kind of water source within this mountain. Without one, Scarlett wasn't sure how much longer she could last. If this dehydration continued, eventually she'd be wishing someone would come along and do her a favor by putting a bullet in her head.

The pathway widened into an open clearing in a basin, the mountains rising up high around her on all sides. Exhausted and bloody, Scarlett tried to scan the area, looking for anything green and growing that might indicate water nearby. Instead, she found something much, much better. About 30 yards away stood a small shack and beside it was a small pond. Scarlett stared at it stupidly for a moment, wondering if she was hallucinating. She staggered forward, dragging her feet further, just a little further, until she reached the edge of the water. Then she collapsed.

The water was colder than she'd expected and the shock to her prickling, pink skin cleared her head. She opened her eyes underwater and saw a small cloud of reddish brown floating away from her feet and chest. *Shit*, she thought. It should have occurred to her to avoid contaminating the only water source she'd seen all day, but it was too late now. And, if Scarlett was being honest with herself, she didn't really care at that exact moment. She opened her mouth, not swallowing, but allowing the water to fill her mouth, swirling around her tongue like a lover's kiss. Her lungs began to ache from the pressure of holding in the stale air, and Scarlett pushed herself up, breaking the surface of the water with a loud gasp. Christ, she really was an easy target. First it was the trail of footprints, and now she wasn't even trying to be quiet. If she didn't get her shit together, she may as well start screaming, "I'M HERE! SHOOT ME!"

Scarlett found she could stand in the manmade pond, the water deep enough to reach her armpits. She squatted down a little, allowing the cool water to cover her sunburnt shoulders. She then cupped her hands in front of her face and slowly sipped the water, careful not to overdo it like she'd done with the canteen. After several sips, Scarlett stopped and tilted her head back, allowing her hair to be fully immersed in the water. Her throat still hurt, but it felt a little better than it had before. As she rested in the water, Scarlett counted out ten minutes, silently ticking the seconds off in her mind, before she slowly picked up her head again and took a few more sips of water. The water felt deliciously cool on her parched lips, and when she was done drinking, she sank down even further into the water, leaving only her head from the nose up above the surface.

Think. She had to think. As tempting as it felt in that moment, Scarlett knew she couldn't stay in the pond forever. If she did, she'd be a sitting duck in a pond—literally. It pained her to do so, but she put her hands on the side of the pond and hoisted herself out of the water, swinging a knee up on the dusty earth beside it. Scarlett didn't mind getting dirty, but it still seemed a shame to end up smeared with dust immediately after rinsing herself off. However, there were certainly more pressing matters at hand, and Scarlett told herself to suck it up and get over it. She gathered her hair and twisted it into a rope, wringing the water out like heavy rain on her foot. Scarlett released her hair and the wet strands stuck to her bare shoulders. Her skin felt better after her dip in the water, but the warmth of the burn was starting to return. Scarlett turned her attention towards the shack and walked gingerly towards it, her feet beginning to bleed again. She momentarily worried about leaving tracks, but remembered the trail of blood she'd already left to the pond. First things first, she had to check the shack for some supplies. She knew the possibility of finding something useful was slim, but she didn't really have any other options. There was also the possibility of finding a person inside the shack and, if the truck in the desert was any indication, people in this desert didn't appear to be particularly friendly.

There was no door on the shack, only an empty frame leading into a cool darkness. Scarlett braced a hand on the doorway and, stepping carefully on her raw feet, she entered the shack.

5

SCARLETT BLINKED, TRYING to force her eyes to adjust to the dark gloom inside the shack. She took a step forward and her legs buckled. Scarlett crashed onto the floor, her knees scraping harshly against the rough wood. There was a sharp prick in her left hand; probably a splinter. Scarlett picked up her hand and squinted at it. The trickle of blood was far too much for a splinter. She carefully lowered her face until her chin was nearly resting on the floor. There, poking out of a wooden plank, was a small nail, its stinger sharp and ready.

"Of course," Scarlett muttered as she picked her head back up, carefully crawling forward and avoiding the nail. Her brain still felt muddled, her focus fading in and out of her mental fog, so she concentrated as hard as she could on not running the nail into her knee. She was so focused, in fact, that she didn't notice the wall of the shed in front of her.

"Ow, shit!" she exclaimed as her head rammed into the metal siding with a bong. Jesus Christ, it really was like she was trying to be found. Just in case the bad guys were too stupid to follow her trail of blood, she was making enough noise to ensure they'd find her. Scarlett instinctively raised her right hand to her head and in doing so, she felt something topple over. The something fell hard on her left fingers, giving her knuckles a heavy smack.

"Fuck!" she growled, yanking her hand free. Scarlett squeezed her fingers as if doing so would stop the pain from spreading, when she realized what had hit her hand: a metal can. Hope caught in her throat as she tentatively picked it up. It fit snugly in her hand and relief flooded her as she read the label in the shadow light: beans. Relief made Scarlett's breath come fast and heavy, and she looked around frantically for a can opener. She saw two more cans of beans and a white jar, but no can opener. Scarlett clutched the can tightly in her hand and half crawled, half dragged herself across the floor towards the doorway of the shed, unwilling to put down the can. She was so desperate for food that the irrational part of her brain was afraid to stop touching the can for even a moment, for fear it would vanish. Logic told her this wasn't possible, but the remnants of drugs still looping through her brain told her otherwise.

Scarlett stuck her head out of the doorway of the shed and looked around, her eyes darting across the ground. She saw a rock the size of her palm with a vaguely formed point on one end and figured that would have to do. She lunged for the rock, warmed from the early afternoon sun, and began banging it against the can of beans, denting the side until it was rumpled and disfigured. For a moment, she wasn't sure if the rock was going to be enough to break through, but she continued to pummel the can until the metal tore, the light brown juice from the beans dribbling over her knuckles. Using her fingers, Scarlett poked and prodded the hole until it was wide enough for a few beans to escape. Then she brought it to her mouth and poured the beans into her mouth, chewing desperately as the juice ran down her chin. Much like the water, Scarlett knew she was in danger of making herself sick if she ate too fast, but she told herself she still had two more cans and if she only ate one, she wouldn't throw up. Probably.

When the can was empty and Scarlett had sucked the last bit of juice that she could from the metal scraps, she backed up enough to get her head inside the shack before she lay down. She struggled to catch her breath, her jaws begging to chew more food. Scarlett told herself that she'd just rest for a little bit, count out the seconds like she did in the pond, and then she could eat more. She closed her eyes as she counted and, before long, she was asleep, cuddling the torn can to her chest like a teddy bear.

6

THE SCOUT DRAGGED herself further down the path, each step getting more and more difficult. The toe of her boot caught on a dip on the ground and she collapsed, narrowly avoiding hitting her nose on the ground. She gingerly put her head down, turning it sideways. Her left eye was now completely swollen shut and the other one was dry and watering. The scout rested, momentarily letting her good eye close. The ground wasn't too bad, all things considered.

Have to get her. Make it right.

The scout forced her eye open, the other one howling in protest. She dragged herself forward, pushing as hard as she could with the toes of her boots. The rocks scraped against her bare stomach and the scout stopped. This wasn't working. She had to get up.

Have to get her. Make it right.

The scout rolled onto her back and nearly screamed in pain. She flipped back to her front as fast as the burning in her belly and side would allow. The scout reached back with tentative, shaking fingers and felt the angry whiplashes across her thighs and backside, still wet under her touch. Her back hurt, but she knew she'd deserved it. The scout pushed herself up on all fours, noticing for the first time that her whole arms, not just her fingers, were streaked and splattered with blood. Hers? She didn't know. If it wasn't all hers, then it was an honor to wear Slaver blood. Grateful tears dripped from her good eye. Kip's blood would be her warpaint, her reminder of what she had to do.

Have to get her. Make it right.

Her right leg buckled slightly when she tried to put weight on it, but the scout forced herself up to as close to a standing position as her body would allow. She hunched forward, her back and limbs bent like a twisted tree. She took a tentative step forward, hopping slightly with the toe of her right boot dragging behind her, drawing a line in the dirt.

Have to get her. Make it right.

The scout took a few more steps, beginning to pick up speed. She wondered vaguely where her rifle went, but it didn't matter. She didn't need it.

Have to get her. Make it right.

The scout took another step forward but her left foot slipped, throwing her balance off and hurling her towards the ground. This time, she didn't catch herself before she hit the ground. This time, the scout's head hit a rock and when her good eye closed, it stayed closed.

7

*S*OMEONE WAS CARRYING *her, their arms were strong and hard. Someone else was talking. Or was it the same person? Scarlett didn't know. She just wanted to sleep.*

"If we don't kill her, she'll come back and find us," Cliff said.

"I can't have her blood on my hands," the vested scout said. Scarlett thought she sounded like Mel, but she was definitely the scout from the desert.

The strong arms loaded her into the back of the Slaver truck, gently setting her down. Scarlett thought the truck should've made noise, but it was silent and soft, like a pillow.

"You'd rather leave it to chance than be sure it's done right?" Cliff asked.

"What other choice is there?" the scout asked. "There ain't nobody here but us naked chickens."

As Scarlett lay in the back of the truck, the scorpion walked over her hand, it's tiny feet tickling her fingers. It was bigger than she remembered, nearly the size of a cat, but much shinier. The color reminded her of a new pair of boots.

"I definitely should've eaten you," Scarlett said.

". . . should've eaten you," Scarlett muttered, her own voice pulling her out of her dream. It took her a moment to realize she wasn't in a truck. She glanced around and slowly recognized the shack. The torn can was still in her hand and Scarlett set it down gently before she propped herself up on her elbow. Her pink skin stung, but her head felt the clearest it had since she woke up in the desert. Scarlett felt like she was starting to get her mental faculties back.

Hello, ladies and gentlemen, nice to see you again, she thought wryly as she organized her thoughts. She sat up gingerly and, as she did so, she winced. Scarlett reached her hand back towards her rear and felt the fine raised lines across her skin. She thought of the path through the mountain, the way it had narrowed. And then she'd heard the shot. She shook her head, not wanting to think about that. There was too much else to focus on, and that woman was probably dead. However, Scarlett wasn't and she wanted to stay that way.

In the fading afternoon light that streamed in through the shack's narrow door frame, Scarlett picked up one of her feet and examined it. She grimaced at the pulverized soles of her feet. She'd known they wouldn't be pretty, but nothing ever really prepared her to examine her own injuries up close. Once, during a mission, Scarlett had taken a bullet in her left arm. Mel had immediately ripped off a piece of her own shirt and tied it tightly around the wound, putting as much pressure on it as she could. Later on, when there was time, a medic had unwrapped Scarlett's arm while an anxious Mel stood by her side. Scarlett had stared with a kind of hypnotic horror at her arm, transfixed by the torn flesh and the layers of skin and muscle in the hole. Mel had thrown up, droplets of vomit splashing the medic's shoes. The medic hadn't had any numbing cream or antiseptic at the time, so he'd had to resort to a more primitive method. He had handed Scarlett a bottle of liquor and she had obediently taken a deep swig, the alcohol burning her throat and pushing tears out of her eyes. The medic had then poured some of the liquor on Scarlett's arm, the fiery liquid burning the wound, and then the medic had dug the bullet out of her bicep. He'd been quick, couldn't have taken longer than 20 seconds or so, but to Scarlett, it had felt like an hour. She'd gripped the side of her chair and gritted her teeth against the screams fighting to get out. Scarlett had felt each tiny movement of the tweezers in her arm, like a metallic insect clawing her from the inside out. She'd desperately wished for Mel to be beside her, holding her hand. Unfortunately, Mel had still been indisposed, by then vomiting into a trash can rather than onto the floor. When the medic finally got hold of the bullet, he pulled it out slowly, sliding it out steadily, and then Scarlett had heard it fall into a metal bowl with a wet clink. The medic had poured some water over the wound, flushing it out as best he could, before wrapping it securely in gauze. Scarlett had momentarily considered asking to keep the bullet, but had instead taken another swig of liquor before collecting Mel. Later, Scarlett learned that after they left the medic, Mel had gone back and retrieved Scarlett's bullet. Mel then drilled a hole in it and strung the bullet on a chain she wore around her neck. Scarlett wondered if Mel still had it or if it'd been tossed out of a truck window as she sped away through the desert.

Scarlett released her foot, not really wanting to look at its mate. She turned her attention to the interior of the shack and glanced around, hoping to find some clothes or at least some linens she could fashion into clothing as well as wraps for her feet. Instead, she saw only the two remaining cans of beans and the white jar. She crawled carefully across the floor to the white jar. She picked it up and examined it, looking for a label of some kind, but found none. She unscrewed the lid and sniffed. Whatever was inside didn't really smell like anything, and Scarlett was disappointed. She'd hoped it was something edible, but when she dug a finger into it, it was creamy and thick like lotion.

Scarlett glanced at her pink shoulder and back to the jar in her hand. *Nothing to lose* Scarlett thought with a painful shrug before she gently touched her lotion-covered finger to her skin. She had half expected the lotion to sting, but instead it provided an instantaneous relief to her skin, cooling her sunburn. Using the tips of her fingers, Scarlett scooped out a little more and began to massage it into her arm in smooth, slow circles. Scarlett squinted at her arm for a moment and then scooted closer towards the door to put her arm in the late afternoon light. Instead of the rosy skin she'd expected to see, her skin had faded back to it's original pale hue. But there was something else different about her arm. It took a second for Scarlett to place it, when she suddenly gasped and grabbed her own arm, twisting it and looking on all sides as if the scar might've run away and set up shop on another part of her body. But the scar from the bullet Scarlett had taken years ago was gone, replaced by smooth, unblemished skin. She glanced back at the jar in astonishment; Scarlett had no idea this even still existed. She'd heard of this kind of healing cream— Christ, what was it called? Every word she wanted seemed to be just out of her mental grasp. Scarlett decided she didn't really care what it was called. As long as she had it and it did what she wanted, then who cared? She crawled back to the jar and methodically began to rub the lotion across every square inch of her skin. She delighted in watching the grooves the rock tunnel had left across her chest when she got stuck fade into nothing but a memory. It was like wiping her skin clean of all its mistakes, restoring it to its original form. The only part of her body she didn't touch was the small tattoo on the inside of her right ankle. She wasn't ready to erase the rune, erase Mel. After they'd been partnering on jobs for over a year, they'd gotten tattooed on a whim. The symbol, which looked like an uppercase "Y" with a small line up the middle, supposedly meant "protection." At least, that's what Mel had said before the tattoo artist in the tavern cut the pattern and painted the ink across their open skin. Whether or not that was accurate had yet to be seen, but after waking up to find herself naked in a desert, Scarlett wasn't in any position to turn down protection.

What had Mel done? Scarlett vaguely remembered her dream and had the notion that there had been something important in it. But all she could think of was the large scorpion. Or had it been a cat? Scarlett wasn't sure and didn't really care either. She'd never put much stock in dreams, viewing them as little more than brain vomit. Mel had always been the one to take her dreams seriously, on occasion backing out of jobs due to some kind of ominous dream she'd had. It drove Scarlett crazy and, as far as she knew, Mel's dreams had never amounted to much of anything other than an annoyance for Scarlett.

Finally, the only area of skin left untouched by the cream other than the tattoo was Scarlett's feet. Although the cream had worked perfectly on the rest of her body, Scarlett was worried that her feet were far too gone, too raw to be fixable with this stuff. But she knew she had no choice and she gingerly touched the lotion to her pulverized soles. As it turned out, she needn't have worried because the sharp ache in her feet vanished almost instantly and after about a minute or so, Scarlett realized she was rubbing the sole of a foot that was smooth and unbroken. She smiled.

When both feet were fixed, there was still half a jar of cream left, so Scarlett replaced the lid and set it aside. She picked up another can of beans and was about to get up to find her pointed rock again, when she noticed the pull tab on the top. She stared at it stupidly for a second before she retrieved the bent and broken can she'd ripped into earlier. Sure enough, one end of the can had a pull tab. Scarlett rolled her eyes and set the empty, ripped can aside.

Don't do drugs, kids, Scarlett thought. *You'll miss what's right in front of your fucking face.*

She returned to the back corner of the shack and peeled back the lid of the second can of beans. She she took her time, slowly chewing the beans as the sun dipped down behind the mountain ridge. The sky turned orange and pink before fading into a deep midnight blue pinpricked with thousands of tiny stars. Scarlett knew she couldn't stay in this shack for long, but for tonight, no one seemed to be using it. She curled up in a corner of the shack, succumbing to the exhaustion that hung heavy in her limbs.

8

SCARLETT AWOKE, STRETCHING out her limbs like a feline. Her foot kicked one of the empty bean cans and she immediately cursed herself. Now, she couldn't even blame the drugs in her system for making her loud and careless. She had to get out of here, and it would be incredibly stupid to draw attention to herself just as she was leaving.

"Shhh!" she admonished the can. It didn't reply, smug and without remorse.

Scarlett stood up and stretched her arms, careful not to accidentally bang her hand on one of the metal walls. She crossed the couple steps to the open doorframe and looked outside, the sky illuminated a pale blue. Scarlett couldn't see the sun's exact position from where she was, but judging by the cooler temperature and the shade of the light, she figured it was early morning, probably near sunrise. She looked at the pond and began to debate with herself about whether or not it was safe to drink.

No, stupid, you bled in the water. That makes it unsafe, she told herself. But would it really be that bad? Her only other alternative was to go without water or to drink her own urine, neither of which sounded appealing. She stood for several minutes, trying to decide which side of the damned if she did, damned if she didn't equation was worse. Finally, she gave in. Scarlett knelt by the pond and cupped her hands, dipping them into the water. At this time of day, the water was cold, colder than Scarlett had expected. The icy water running down her throat made her shiver for just a second and when she was done, she stood up and shook the spare water droplets off her hands. The drops flew from her fingers and onto the surface of the pond, creating ripples that ringed their way to the edges of the water. She watched them for a moment, enjoying the serenity of the water's dance. When it was done, she turned to go back inside the shack.

That was when she saw her.

Were it not for the outfit of a black vest, loincloth, and boots, Scarlett might not have recognized the scout from the truck. Half of her face was swollen, one eye completely closed, and what looked like dried blood was caked on her face around a broken nose. She was limping, and there were bruises and lacerations across her body. The scout held a small rock in one hand and was swaying dangerously from side to side, like the top of a tree in high wind.

"Haffa . . . get you . . . may rye," the scout mumbled, barely able to get the words out of her bruised, purple face. The scout tried to raise the hand with the rock in it, but the effort seemed too great and the hand dropped back to her side.

"What are you going to do, throw that at me?" Scarlett asked with a snort. "You can barely stand up."

The scout looked at the rock in her hand and then back to Scarlett.

"Fuck you, bitch," the scout said, only it came out sounding more like, "Fuff ooh, bish." And then the scout promptly passed out, crashing down to her knees with twin puffs of dust before pitching face first into the dirt. Scarlett stared at the scout lying motionless on the ground and put her hands on her hips.

"Well, fuck," Scarlett said aloud. She walked over to the scout and circled her for a moment, evaluating. There were oozing lacerations on the back of her legs, so Scarlett knew she didn't want to flip her over, but it was exactly polite to drag someone facedown either. In the end, Scarlett picked up the scout's arms, lifting them high enough to pull her face off the ground, and dragged her into the shack.

9

SCARLETT DROPPED THE woman on the floor, the scout's head hitting the wood with a dull thunk. Scarlett knelt beside her and leaned closer to the wounds on the woman's legs and buttocks, examining them more thoroughly. Were those whip marks? God, that would explain the screaming Scarlett had heard. Really, everything about this woman's appearance explained the screaming. What her presence didn't explain, however, was the gunshot. Scarlett had assumed that the bullet had been for the scout, but evidently not. The chick had a lot of wounds, but a gunshot wound wasn't one of them. Did that mean one of the two men that chased her were dead? Were they both dead? Did someone else show up? Scarlett hated that she had to care about these questions when all she wanted were some goddamn clothes, but perhaps that would be fixed momentarily.

Scarlett sat back and evaluated the woman's clothes. They weren't much, but they were better than nothing. Scarlett went for the boots first, her fingers tugging at the knotted laces, pulling them free so she could slip the scout's boots off of her feet. Relieved,

Scarlett took one of the boots and jammed her own foot inside.

Her foot made it about halfway, and then stopped.

The shoes were too tight, at least two sizes too small, but Scarlett didn't want to admit defeat. She pushed and pulled and did everything she could to cajole her foot into the boot, but it refused to budge. Frustration bubbled up inside her, but she closed her eyes and forced it down with a few measured breaths. *Good air in, pissed off air out. Good air in, pissed off air out.*

Scarlett set the boots aside for a moment and examined the loin cloth. It appeared to be sewn onto the woman, leather straps tightly sutured to prevent it from ever being taken off without being cut off. Scarlett considered that she might be able to saw through the leather strap with a sharp rock, but the scout was a little smaller than her and there would be no way for Scarlett to secure it to her own body. Screw it. Scarlett would leave the scout with a little dignity.

Scarlett then turned her attention to the vest. It wasn't as good as a shirt, but at least it'd provide better sun protection for her shoulders than her hair. She carefully maneuvered the unconscious scout's arms out of the thick leather vest and tugged it free from underneath her prone body. Scarlett stood up and slid one arm in, and then the other, and then found herself unable to pull her shoulders forward. Her shoulder blades were pinned back by the vest, far too tight to be worn comfortably. Scarlett tried in vain to force her arms forward, but they bounced back under the unyielding black leather.

"Fuck!" Scarlett growled through her teeth, thoroughly exasperated. "God dammit."

Scarlett took off the vest and dropped it on the floor beside the scout. Apparently, clothes for Scarlett simply weren't in the cards today. She picked up the last can of beans and was about to leave when she glanced back at the scout. A woman who had once been fearsome, standing upright in the back of a truck with a gun, shooting at Scarlett, now looked so small and beaten and helpless. *Not my problem,* Scarlett told herself as she turned to leave. But then she looked back again. Scarlett sighed. If she couldn't take the scout's clothes, the least she could do would be to put them back on her. Leaving someone naked in the desert wasn't Scarlett's style.

Scarlett knelt beside the scout and set down the can of beans. She shoved the boots roughly onto the scout's feet, not bothering to tie them. Then she slid the vest back on to the scout's shoulders. As she did so, Scarlett noticed for the first time the thick black collar around the woman's neck. How had she missed that? She pushed the scout's hair aside and leaned in to get a better look at the collar. It was tight, not even enough space for Scarlett to slide a finger between the collar and the scout's neck, and at the back, hidden underneath her hair, was a heavy lock. Scarlett let go of the woman and looked at the collar for a long time, wondering what exactly she'd wandered into.

Scarlett reached for the jar of cream and unscrewed the lid, setting the metal top aside. She gently applied the cream on the lacerations on the scout's buttocks before taking care of the various other cuts and bruises along the backs of her legs. Then Scarlett flipped the woman over, careful to avoid the exposed nail in the floor, and took care of the scout's front. By the time Scarlett got to the scout's face, the jar was nearly empty. Scarlett dragged the tips of her fingers around the bottom rim of the jar, scraping up whatever little bit of cream she could get, and applied it to the woman's face. It wasn't quite enough to take care of all of the bruising and swelling, but at least she'd be able to open her eye. The woman's face was covered in a Rorschach spattering of blood and something thicker that Scarlett was fairly certain she recognized. She considered filling the now empty jar and using it to clean off the scout's face, but Scarlett knew that would probably wake her up and, frankly, Scarlett didn't care that much. She'd done her good deed for the day.

Suddenly, the scout stirred in her sleep. Scarlett immediately yanked one of the boot laces free from its shoe and bound the scout's hands. She then took the second bootlace and threaded it through the eyes of both boots, linking them together. Was it a great long term solution? No, of course not, but at least this would slow her down long enough so Scarlett could put some distance between her and the scout, boots or no boots. But the scout merely relaxed again, her face rolling sleepily to one side, and she began to snore lightly, no louder than a cat's purr.

Scarlett stood up. She'd lallygagged enough. It was time to get the fuck out.

Scarlett had barely stepped outside the shack when she heard the truck. Fuck, the two men who had been with the scout weren't gone after all. She looked back at the scout. Scarlett was pretty sure that the men she'd been with were the ones that had beaten her up. Leaving her behind was likely a death sentence, but Scarlett wasn't about to flip the scout over her shoulder and carry her off. Besides, the bitch had technically tried to kill her on more than one occasion. Scarlett turned and crept out of the shack. She heard the truck pull up behind the shack and the engine cut off. Scarlett listened intently as two voices got out of the truck, slamming the doors behind them. They were walking around the left side of the shack so Scarlett went right, stepping as carefully and as silently as she could. She peeked around the back of the shack and saw an empty truck. As long as she could give the two voices a location, she might be able to avoid them long enough to get away. Maybe even take the truck.

"What the fuck?" a woman's voice said. Scarlett heard the heavy footfalls of boots on the wooden floor inside the metal shack walls. "Is that a *slave*?"

Ah, Scarlett thought. *Explains the collar.*

"Looks like it," a male voice replied. "Want me to shoot her?"

"Not yet," the female voice replied. "A slave in our territory is bound to know something. She might be useful. Throw her in the truck."

"Looks like someone already did us a favor by restraining her," the male voice said.

Scarlett heard shuffling and a grunt as the male voice picked up the still unconscious scout.

"What the *fuck*?" the female voice asked again, much louder and angrier this time. The glass jar smashed against other side of the wall, making Scarlett flinch. "Oh, this bitch is gonna die for sure," the woman growled.

Scarlett listened as the voices came out of the shack. Left or right? Right. Scarlett scooted around the back of the shack and circled away from the voices as they headed for the truck. Scarlett heard a loud thump and imagined the scout's body dropping heavily in the back of the truck like a sack of potatoes. She heard both truck doors open and then the engine awakened with a grumble. Scarlett let out a slow breath she hadn't realized she'd been holding. As soon as they left, she could go too.

"Come on, man, hurry up, we gotta go!" the male voice yelled from the direction of the truck. Suddenly, two strong, burly arms wrapped around Scarlett from behind and picked her up before slamming her into the ground. Scarlett's head hit the ground with an unnerving whack but she didn't lose consciousness. The two arms picked her up again and threw her over a muscular shoulder and carried her to the truck. Scarlett was unceremoniously dropped into the back of the vehicle beside the scout and her head hit the truck bed. As the blackness around her vision faded in towards a pinpoint before overtaking her completely, Scarlett saw the arms that had grabbed her were attached to a big man who hopped into the truck bed and raised the gate. Just before she lost consciousness, she saw a red feather similar to the one she'd seen on the sign in the desert hanging from a leather cord around his neck.

Fucking feather, she thought. And then she didn't think anything at all.

10

THE MOTORBIKES HUMMED like an angry swarm of wasps through the desert. The noise felt appropriate to Grun as he gripped the vibrating handlebars of his bike because he was angry. Very angry. That little pissant Crick had come back alone with a beat up truck and a missing slave. Grun didn't appreciate seeing bullet holes in one of his trucks. He didn't like the idea of lost property, especially if the property in question had run into Eagle territory. Grun knew that the Eagles weren't stupid—they were likely going to interrogate that stupid bitch before they killed her. If she had any semblance of brains in her head, she'd keep her goddamn mouth shut and not betray them to the Eagles. But if she didn't . . . well, Grun didn't like the idea of his to do list getting any longer today.

The bikes closed in on the Coahuila sign and Grun brought his bike to a stop, signaling for the others to do the same. The Slavers obediently cut the power on their bikes and silence settled around them.

"Clear it," he muttered to the woman in the sidecar of his bike. She immediately hopped out, dressed only in boots and her helmet with a rifle in hand, and immediately crouched down, sighting the gun. As she swept the scope across the rock face, Grun took a moment to admire her animalistic movements as he ran a hand over his shaved head. She looked almost feral, like a desert cat, her body tanned and strong in the late afternoon sun.

The woman stood up and lowered the gun. She turned her head towards Grun and nodded.

"Good girl," Grun said as he climbed off of his bike. He walked around behind her and smacked her twice on her rear end, the second time digging his fingers into her skin. Hard. She didn't so much as turn her head when he did so. Grun smirked. The Pet didn't breathe, eat, or shit without his permission.

Just the way he liked it.

Grun circled around The Pet and looked at the sight before him. Only this time, he wasn't looking at the Coahuila sign. Instead, he was looking beside it. There was a new post in the ground, tightly secured in the dry desert earth. Grun let his eyes travel up the post, his eyes tracing the dark, reddish brown lines that had dripped down. At the top of the post, Grun saw Kip's head—or, at least, what was left of it. The top left quadrant was missing, blasted off in a raw, coagulated maw of blood and brain mattered splintered with bone fragments. The eye that was still present was obscured from view, caked with dried blood. The cut across Kip's neck was jagged, like someone had sawed it roughly before jamming it atop the spike.

Fucking idiot.

Behind him, Grun heard someone retch. Grun turned around slowly, motioning for The Pet to do the same.

"Does someone not like what they see?" Grun asked lightly. No one said a word, but Grun saw a small movement out of the corner of his eye. In a flash, The Pet had her rifle on her shoulder and pointed at the man in the back of the group who had the back of his hand pressed tightly to his lips. The Pet looked askance at Grun who shook his head slightly. She lowered the rifle, but only just. Grun began to walk through the group, making his way towards Hawk, the man in the back. Grun strode slowly, almost casually, his footfalls sounding obscenely loud in the silent desert. He stopped inches away from Hawk, who averted his eyes down to Grun's boots. Hawk was a big man, but Grun was bigger, the sun glistening on his bare arms.

"Since when do you have such a weak constitution?" Grun asked. His voice sounded pleasant enough, but there was a dangerous, sharp undertone to his words.

Hawk said nothing.

Grun leaned a little closer, listening intently. The son of a bitch was holding his breath. Grun wondered momentarily if it'd be worth it to make Hawk piss himself, but decided that was an amusement he didn't have time for. He turned to leave the sniveling little sack of shit, but changed his mind and whirled around, landing his fist against Hawk's face. Grun felt Hawk's nose crunch underneath his knuckles and smiled as the man collapsed across his motorbike.

"Suck it up, sunshine," Grun growled. "I don't have time for this shit."

Grun walked back to the front of the group where The Pet was waiting for him. He couldn't see her eyes under the helmet, but he knew they were on him.

"Anyone else?" Grun asked brightly, turning to survey the rest of the group. The rest of the Slavers said nothing, staring straight ahead as the sweat beaded on their bare heads and chests. Grun looked back to Kip's decapitated head sitting atop the spike. Then he saw something else, something he hadn't noticed before. Dangling below Kip's neck, streaked with dark, dried blood, were red and yellow feathers. Grun stared at the feathers for a long time, unmoving. Without warning, he lashed out his boot, kicking the post fiercely. There was a crack that split the tense quiet of the landscape, but the post didn't break. However, Kip's head popped off the spike, shooting up about a foot or so before it fell down to the ground, bouncing once on the whole side of Kip's skull before it rolled to a stop like a defective ball. Grun looked out past Kip's head to a spot in the dirt up ahead, dark sprays arcing across the earth. Grun stared at the spots for a long time before he turned back to his men, awaiting their next order.

"We're going to war, boys."

He couldn't see The Pet's face, no one could, but as she stood beside him, Grun could have sworn he felt her smile.

11

*A*N ENGINE RUMBLED beneath Scarlett like the purr of a cat. She heard voices, indistinct at first, and then clearer.

"Where are we going?" Cliff asked.

"You know where," Mel replied, her voice flat and emotionless.

"I thought you were kidding."

"Why would I joke about Coahuila?"

"Because . . . Jesus, Mel."

"You're the one that wanted to kill her outright."

"This is way more fucked up, and you know it," Cliff insisted.

"I can't just kill her."

"That's basically what you're doing if we—"

"Shut up, Cliff."

"Mel, you know I'm—"

"Shut the FUCK up, Cliff!" Mel yelled.

Scarlett suddenly saw Mel's face hovering over hers. But it wasn't quite right. Scarlett wondered why Mel looked like that psychopathic scout and had red and yellow feathers in her hair.

The truck hit a bump and jostled Scarlett out of her dream, tossing her up slightly before slamming her back down on to the hard bed of the truck. The side of Scarlett's head hit the metal, pain flaring across her skull like a raging brushfire.

"Ow, fuck," Scarlett groaned. She tried to raise a hand to her head, but was surprised to find they were stuck behind her back. Still wincing, Scarlett craned her neck to look over her shoulder and saw the length of rope that wound tightly around her wrists and bound them to her ankles.

"Oh, what the fuck is this shit?" Scarlett asked, irritated. She looked around the truck and saw a large, burly man sitting in the corner by the truck bed's tailgate. He didn't acknowledge Scarlett's somewhat rhetorical question. The man wore brown pants and woven leather armor over his torso. Around his neck hung a red feather on a leather cord. That fucking feather—it was coming back to her now. She recalled seeing that just before she passed out. And before that . . . ah, yes. Scarlett remembered everything: the shack, the people in the truck, the cream—oh, shit. One of her delightful new captors had been rather upset about that cream. Scarlett remembered the sound of glass breaking when the woman had smashed the jar inside the shack, the shards tinkling down like raindrops. Whatever was happening to Scarlett now, she knew it wasn't good. As if waking up hogtied in a truck while being guarded by a big, muscled man wasn't enough of a red flag.

Scarlett lay the side of her head back down on the bed of the truck. Each bump of the ride made her headache worse, but it strained her neck too much to keep her head raised while she was tied in this position. Beside her lay the unconscious scout, tied in a similar fashion with her hand behind her back, wrists bound to ankles. Scarlett thought back to the men in the desert, the ones whom she'd seen with the scout. Obviously, if the scout was tied up, this was a different tribe of people . . . right? The men from before had worn black pants and vests and had been bare chested with shaved heads. They had looked severe and unrelenting. Based on the condition in which the scout had stumbled out of the tunnel, Scarlett figured it was safe to assume that those men in black weren't exactly the warm and fuzzy type who were looking for a cuddle. The man sitting in the truck, however, was different. He didn't look particularly cuddly either, but there was something more relaxed, more natural about him. His clothing seemed to fit the landscape, almost blending in like he belonged in the desert, whereas the other men had stood out, accentuating the sharp, dry hardness of the desert. Considering everyone seemed hellbent on capturing her, Scarlett wasn't particularly fond of either group, but at least these people didn't try to shoot her on sight, so that seemed like a plus.

The truck suddenly slammed on its brakes and Scarlett and the scout shot forward, their bodies still in motion until their heads hit the back of the cab as well as each other.

"Motherfucker!" Scarlett growled through gritted teeth, the sickening sound of skull thudding against skull echoing in her ears. The scout, still unconscious, said nothing. The pain made Scarlett angry and she pulled against her restraints, but the rope held fast. It barely even moved across her skin. Whomever had tied this had clearly done this before. Unlucky for Scarlett as that meant it would be that much more difficult to break free, but she'd be less likely to rub her wrists raw in the process. Nothing like Mel. Mel was a hell of a mercenary, but she had no fucking clue what she was doing when it came to knots. Scarlett had attempted to improve Mel's knot tying skills, but Mel had made little to no progress.

"Hopeless," Scarlett would admonish, rolling her eyes. But Mel never really seemed bothered by it, shrugging off Scarlett's comments like an old coat.

"I don't like that sort of language."

Scarlett picked up her head and strained her neck to look towards the man at the other end of the truck bed, who had stood up and was dropping the tailgate.

"What?" Scarlett asked, confused. She had wanted to say "what the fuck?" but thought it best to not be intentionally petulant while tied up in such a compromising position.

"I don't like that sort of language," the man repeated, looking Scarlett in the eye for the first time since she'd awoken in the back of the truck.

"I apologize if my manners aren't up to snuff, but is this really the best time to discuss my verbal etiquette?" Scarlett asked.

So much for watching her attitude.

The man didn't reply. Instead, he hopped out of the truck and onto the ground. Then he reached out and grasped both Scarlett's bindings and the scout's, one in each hand, and yanked hard. Scarlett gritted her teeth as her body slid across the length of the truck bed, seeming to catch every small rock that had been inadvertently kicked in there. The dirt rasped against her skin like sandpaper and Scarlett found herself wishing for what felt like the hundredth time that she had a pair of pants or a shirt. The man slung the scout over one of his broad shoulders and heaved Scarlett over the other, hanging on to both women by their knees. Scarlett grunted when her face hit the man's back, solid as a rock wall.

"Rude," she said, her voice muffled by the man's back. If he heard her, he ignored her.

Scarlett strained her neck to get a look around and she saw that the man was carrying them into a dark cave. She couldn't see anyone walking behind them so she assumed the other two people were walking in front. The further they moved into the cave, the lower the temperature dropped. Scarlett could feel goosebumps ripple across her exposed flesh and she wondered exactly how far in they were going to go. Then the light started to return, slowly at first, but then it grew and grew and Scarlett could once again see a little bit. But the light was muted, definitely not the mid-morning sun they'd left behind outside the cave.

The man unceremoniously dropped Scarlett and the scout on the ground in twin heaps. Scarlett let out something close to a growl when she slammed onto the floor of the cave on her side, her hands still tied tightly behind her back. She shook the stars from her eyes and glanced around the cave, seeing torches posted around the open space. Tied at the base of each torch was a string of red and yellow feathers.

"Was that necessary?" Scarlett asked the big man who had been carrying her. He smirked and walked to the side. Scarlett saw two more people standing before her, a woman and a man, the latter a smaller version of the one who had tossed Scarlett around like a ragdoll.

"What do you want me to do with that one, Brenna?" the smaller man asked, pointing to the scout.

"Nothing for now," Brenna said, taking a couple steps closer to Scarlett. Scarlett noticed that the woman was tall, with ramrod straight posture. Her hair was cropped short and the sleeveless shirt she wore underneath her own woven chest armor exposed tough, sinewy arms. "When she wakes up, she might know something useful. Then again, maybe not. You know how fucked in the head those slaves are."

Puzzle pieces clicked into place in Scarlett's brain, but she pushed the information aside for now, storing it for later.

"You, on the other hand," Brenna said to Scarlett, "are not wearing a collar. Nor do you have the brand, and you have your hair, so I'm assuming you're not like you're friend here."

"I don't belong to anyone," Scarlett said evenly, although Mel's face briefly flashed across her mind.

"And yet here you are, inconveniencing my day," Brenna said.

"Inconveniencing *your* day?" Scarlett asked. "Your goon slams me into the ground like a sack of laundry, I wake up hogtied in the back of a truck, and then I'm dragged into a goddamn cave, and I'm inconveniencing *your* day?"

Brenna swiftly knelt beside Scarlett and grabbed a fistful of her hair. She yanked it, hard. Scarlett wanted to cry out but she stifled it behind gritted teeth.

"What were you doing out there in the desert anyway?" Brenna asked, her polite tone belying the vice-like grip she had on Scarlett's hair. "Sunbathing?"

"Yes, I thought I'd get a jump start on my tan for summer," Scarlett said sweetly. "Not all of us are born as naturally beautiful as you, some of us have to work at it."

Brenna delivered a sharp kick to Scarlett's hip. Scarlett grunted, but didn't cry out.

"It seems that while you were goofing around, you took something that didn't belong to you," Brenna said, winding Scarlett's hair a little tighter around her hand. "Something very valuable."

"If it was so valuable, you probably shouldn't have forgotten it in that shack like an idiot," Scarlett retorted. Jesus Christ, she had to shut up and stop mouthing off.

Brenna pulled Scarlett up by her hair and slapped her across the face with her free hand. The smack echoed slightly in the cave and Scarlett's cheek stung like a sunburn.

"Fucking cunt," Brenna spat.

"He doesn't like that sort of language," Scarlett muttered, gesturing towards the big man who had carried her with her eyes as she wondered if her cheek would swell. *Oh my god, SHUT UP!*

"Why, you stupid—" Brenna said, cocking her hand to slap Scarlett again.

"You can't leave a mark."

Brenna stopped and looked over at the big man, standing casually off to the side.

"I'm sorry to speak out of turn, Captain, but you can't leave a mark. You know the law."

Brenna gave a disgusted sigh and let go of Scarlett's hair, dropping her back onto the cave floor.

"Yes, I know," Brenna said, sounding disappointed. But then a thought occurred to her. "However, we have ways around that," Brenna said, her face twisting as she glared at Scarlett until it formed a semblance of a smile.

Me and my stupid fucking mouth.

Brenna pulled a flogger from her belt and ran her fingers through the leather straps as she began to slowly pace in front of Scarlett.

"What about this?" Brenna asked lightly. "Would this leave a mark? Or do you think it would heal in time before anyone saw you?" she mused.

Scarlett watched her warily, twisting her neck uncomfortably to look up at Brenna. God, Scarlett hated that sanctimonious smirk on Brenna's face.

"No, probably not," Brenna said, sounding disappointed. "Maybe we have another option," Brenna continued, turning to the large man who was watching her with unamused eyes. "Do we—"

Brenna's question was cut off by the sound of rapid footsteps. The footsteps grew louder and they finally stopped, replaced by heavy panting. Scarlett twisted on the ground until she could see a man standing in the entrance to the cave, dressed similarly to the others, with a yellow feather dangling off of his wrist.

Excellent, another one, Scarlett thought, rolling her eyes.

"Captain," the new arrival said. "It's the Slavers. The Elders need to see everyone immediately."

Brenna groaned, annoyed.

"Now?" she asked.

The man nodded.

"Now," he confirmed.

Brenna tucked the flogger back into her belt.

"Well, let's go then. Bring the trash," Brenna said, gesturing to Scarlett and the scout.

"Aww, I love the nickname," Scarlett said. "Maybe later we can braid each other's hair."

Brenna said nothing, but kicked Scarlett in the stomach, hard. Scarlett wheezed, gasping for air as the big man hauled her up over his shoulder again.

Worth it.

12

THE DOOR TO the inner sanctum hit the wall with a loud crack as four Slavers dragged in the two Eagle scouts. The Eagles were bloody and beaten, their faces streaked with blood and dirt. The Slavers dropped them on the ground and they landed on all fours, their knees thudding dully on impact. Grun settled back casually in his chair as he watched the two men panting on the ground, a thin string of bloody saliva hanging from one of the scout's mouths.

"Found them towards the back of the compound," one of the Slavers said.

A thin smile played across Grun's lips, but his eyes remained cold. Beside him, The Pet stood rigidly at attention, her rifle slung across her back.

"Well," Grun said. "It appears you fellas have wandered into the wrong sandbox, doesn't it?"

The Eagles said nothing, not even daring to raise their eyes.

"You boys have put me in a bit of an awkward situation," Grun said casually as he examined his nails. The lines of dirt beneath the nails reminded him a little of his favorite knife's curved blade. He pulled the knife in question from his belt and used the tip to clear out his fingernail homages. "See, you're forcing me to make a difficult choice here. Don't get me wrong, I want to kill you," he said as he flicked his eyes up to the pair before him. "There's nothing I enjoy more than watching the life drain out of an Eagle's eyes—well, if they still have eyes at that point," Grun amended, laughing at his own joke. The other Slavers joined in, their laughter ricocheting off the narrow walls of the inner sanctum. The Pet didn't make a sound, standing so still she could have been stone. Grun held up his hand and the Slavers immediately stopped laughing, their guffaws cut off mid-breath.

"I'm faced with a bit of a conundrum here," Grun continued. "Do I kill you? Do I send you back to deliver my message to your leaders? If I do the latter, do I really need to send two of you? One person could deliver it just fine, especially if I carve it into your arm. Or your back. Or your face. Two messengers just seems excessive."

Grun tapped his chin with the flat side of his knife, striking an overly thoughtful pose.

"I suppose I could just pick one of you to kill and get it over with," Grun said. "But that kind of takes the fun out of it, don't you think? I mean, yes, it's effective, but there's no theater in it, no sport."

An idea occurred to Grun and he sat up a little straighter in his chair and leaned forward, tossing his knife on the ground in front of the Eagle scouts.

"I'm going to give you two choices," Grun said, resting his elbows on his knees. "One, you two can fight to the death with my knife here and the winner gets to leave. Or two," Grun said, gesturing to The Pet to give him her gun, which she did obediently, "you can both fight her." Grun pointed at The Pet. "If you kill her, you can both leave. I still think two messengers is a bit redundant, but I suppose that's the ticket price of a good show."

The two Eagle scouts tentatively raised their heads to look at The Pet. She was clearly in good shape, not an ounce of fat on her naked body, but she was small and thin. One on one, she might put up a formidable fight, but two on one? Unlikely. The helmet that covered her whole head was a little unnerving and reminiscent of an executioner, but the helmet wasn't the part of her that was going to be throwing punches.

"Your choice gentlemen," Grun said.

One of the Eagle scouts raised his bleeding hand and pointed towards The Pet.

"Well, then let the games begin," Grun said, his face breaking out into a broad grin as he leaned The Pet's rifle against the arm of his chair.

For a moment, no one moved. Then one of the Eagle scouts reached out a trembling hand for the knife. Before his fingertips had barely brushed the knife's wooden handle, The Pet seized hold of his arm, cracking his elbow backwards over her knee. The Eagle screamed in pain and fell back to the floor. The second Eagle grabbed for The Pet's ankle but she stomped on his fingers, pinning him in place as she delivered a nose-breaking blow to his face. The first Eagle pulled himself to his feet and lunged at her, but The Pet sidestepped him easily. As he fell past her, The Pet reached out and caught his head between her hands, snapping his neck as easily as she had his arm. The remaining Eagle climbed to his knees, blinking the blood from his eyes and swaying a little from the hit to his head. Grun stood up from his chair and took a couple steps to reach the Eagle, bending over until their eyes were level.

"Probably should've picked the first choice, huh?" Grun asked with a smirk.

The Eagle didn't say anything. Then he mustered up what little strength he had left and spit in Grun's face, spraying him with rosy saliva. Grun stood up and calmly wiped his face with his hand, flinging the moisture off to the side with a shake of his fingers.

"You can spit all you want, but that won't change your fate," Grun said. "Or your people's fate. The Eagles have crossed me for the last time and this time, I'm going to level them to the ground."

Grun nodded at The Pet who instantly sprang into action. She grabbed the knife and cut a gash in the Eagle's neck. Then she dropped the knife and ripped out the inside of his throat with her bare hands. The Eagle's eyes bulged and he fell to the floor, twitching as the last of his life faded away. Then, he was still.

Grun bent down and picked up his knife from where The Pet had dropped it. He wiped the blade off on his black pants and returned the knife to his belt. Grun stepped over the dead Eagle and into a pool of blood. The Pet followed closely, only one step behind, and together their boots left twin trails on the floor as they headed towards the door. The other Slavers who had been watching the display immediately jumped aside, the ones closest to The Pet taking an additional step backwards, their backs bumping against the wall.

"Get someone to clean up that fucking mess," Grun ordered. "But save their heads."

13

SCARLETT LAY ON her side, examining her fellow captive. After the arrival of the runner, Scarlett and the scout had been dumped unceremoniously into the back of truck again. God, she still hadn't woken up yet, despite getting thrown around like a ragdoll by the boulder who was passing himself off as a man. Was the scout dead? Scarlett wasn't sure. The truck was bouncing enough to where Scarlett couldn't watch the rise and fall of the scout's chest to check her breathing. Instead, she turned her attention to her captor.

"So, come here often?" Scarlett asked, straining her neck so she could see him seated at the back of the truck.

He ignored her.

"How long have you been in the business of kidnapping? Judging by these knots, probably a while. These aren't amateur knots, that's for sure," Scarlett continued.

This time he glanced at her, but still he said nothing.

"I have a question, do you feel like knot tying is something you can teach? I mean, really good knot tying. I tried to teach someone once and she was just awful at it. Granted, that might have been a personal issue, but maybe you're just born with an inherent knot tying ability. Like being naturally athletic, but with . . . fingers," Scarlett said, trailing off a little as she put her temple back down on the bed of the truck. She wasn't entirely sure where she'd been going with that. However, she had taken several hits to the head lately, so the blame for her lack of mental faculties couldn't entirely fall on her.

"Maybe you're just a terrible teacher," the man said.

Scarlett picked her head up again and looked at him. He wasn't looking at her, but she was sure she'd heard him. Scarlett considered his comment for a moment.

"Nah, good knot tying definitely takes natural ability," she finally said.

"If you say so," the man said, still looking out over the horizon instead of at her.

"So, do you have a name?" Scarlett asked. She wasn't entirely sure why she felt so hellbent on making conversation with him. There was a theory that one way to help yourself out in captivity was to make yourself appear more human to your captors. They'd be less likely to kill you or something if you appealed to their human side. Scarlett had never had much of a use for this technique; on the rare occasion she'd been caught, she'd simply left a trail of bodies in her wake. Maybe her captors should've spent some time humanizing themselves to her.

The midday sun beat down on them, and Scarlett felt like she was baking in the truck bed. Her skin was starting to burn and she found herself wishing for more of that cream. Then again, that was part of what had gotten her hogtied in a truck. Scarlett opened her mouth and was about to ask the man another question when she suddenly heard the crack of a bullet break through the air. The man immediately dropped down, landing hard on top of Scarlett and the scout.

"Ow, fuck!" Scarlett exclaimed. Despite the sound of bullets peppering the air, the man still turned his head to glare at her. "Okay, I know you don't like that kind of language, but Jesus Christ, man, you're really heavy!"

His expression didn't change, but he moved slightly to take some of his weight off of her.

"Thanks," Scarlett said.

"Slaver ambush!" Brenna yelled back over her shoulder through the open window leading into the truck cab. "We have a few trucks waiting for us up ahead if we can make it to that outcrop up there."

The man in the truck bed lifted himself up slightly to survey the scene and then dropped back down between Scarlett and the scout.

"Can we make it?" he yelled back.

"We're gonna find out," Brenna replied. "Get ready."

The man popped his head back up for a moment before he ducked down once more. He pulled a knife from his belt and reached for Scarlett. She held her breath for a moment and braced herself, waiting for the cut, but then she felt something else behind her. She strained to look over her shoulder and saw that he was cutting her feet free. When he was done, he reached over and quickly did the same to the scout.

"What are you doing?" Scarlett asked, surprised.

"It's not very honorable to leave women tied up when Slavers are around," he said.

"What about my hands?" Scarlett asked hopefully.

"I'm giving you a chance, not an advantage," he replied.

Scarlett groaned and rolled on to her back, exasperated. But even with her bound wrists creating an uncomfortable hump behind her back, she still enjoyed the feeling of being able to stretch out her legs.

"Néron."

"What?" Scarlett asked as she flexed her feet.

"My name is Néron," the man said.

"Scarlett," she said. "I'd shake your hand, but *someone* made that a little difficult."

Just then, Brenna slammed on the brakes and all three passengers in the truck bed shot forward. Néron caught himself with his hands, but both Scarlett and the scout slammed into the back of the cab headfirst.

"Ow, shit!" Scarlett exclaimed. Néron gave her one more withering glare before he jumped over the side of the truck bed. Beside her, the scout groaned, making her first noise in hours. Well, apparently she wasn't dead after all. The scout's eyes fluttered open.

"Good morning, darling," Scarlett said drily. "Nice of you to join the party."

"What . . . where . . ." the scout asked before her words shattered into a cough.

Scarlett began to scoot along the truck bed towards the tailgate. As long as it wasn't locked, she figured she'd be able to get the latch with her foot. She considered sitting up and using her hands, but if people were firing guns around here, that seemed like a very stupid idea unless she wanted a bullet in her skull. As if to illustrate her point, a bullet whizzed overhead. Several more responded.

"Hey . . ." the scout said slowly as she looked down the length of the truck bed at Scarlett, recognition slowly permeating her thoughts. "Hey!"

Scarlett quickly worked her foot into the latch and pulled her knee towards her chest, popping it open. The tailgate fell with a clang. Out of the corner of her eye, Scarlett saw something coming towards her head and she rolled away, just barely avoiding the scout's kick.

"Get back here!" the scout yelled at her. Scarlett ignored the order and rolled out of the back of the truck, landing on her back and hands, the wind rushing out of her in a hard gust. Her shoulders screamed in protest and she struggled to catch her breath, but Scarlett knew she couldn't stay there. She rolled on to her stomach and pushed herself up on her knees, using her forehead for balance until she had both knees underneath her. Scarlett glanced over at the scout, but found she was sitting up and no longer looking in Scarlett's direction.

"Hey!" the scout yelled, looking towards the people in the distance who were advancing on the outcrop like an ominous black cloud. "Hey! Over here!"

"What the fuck are you doing?" Scarlett yelled at the scout.

"They came back for me! Hey! I'm here!" the scout called again, climbing to her feet.

Scarlett stared at her in disbelief for a moment.

"Fucking idiot," Scarlett said before she turned and hurried behind one of the large rocks. Think, think, she had to think. She needed to get as far away from this clusterfuck as possible, but she had no idea where she was. Scarlett scanned the landscape and a couple miles away, she could see some hills. That'd have to do. Scarlett glanced around to check the location of the encroaching army and saw more trucks driving in from the side. They were relatively far away, but even from this distance Scarlett thought she could see them dressed similarly to Néron and Brenna. Reinforcements, of course. *Duh, Scarlett* she thought. If she was going to make a run for it, the time was now. Scarlett broke into a run, hands still tied behind her back. Her feet hurt and she found herself wishing again for boots. Hell, she'd even take a pair of socks at this point. She had nearly cleared the outcrop when suddenly something slammed into her from behind, knocking her down, hard.

"Where do you think you're going?" a familiar voice asked with a snarl.

14

A HAND GRIPPED Scarlett's arm and flipped her onto her back, turning her face to face with Brenna.

"I'm not done with you, you thieving cunt," Brenna hissed at her.

"I don't know, I feel like we've had so much fun already that I'm not sure how much more I can handle," Scarlett said.

Brenna glanced down at Scarlett's ankles.

"How did . . . oh, god dammit, Néron," Brenna muttered, answering her own question before she focused back on Scarlett's face. "Well too fucking bad, princess, it looks like we're going to—"

The rest of her words were cut off by a loud explosion. Seizing the moment, Scarlett brought both knees to her chest and kicked Brenna in the stomach as hard as she could. Caught off guard, Brenna stumbled backwards and fell on the ground, giving Scarlett enough time to climb to her feet and take off running again, circling around the outcrop. As she ran, Scarlett wiggled her wrists and found that they were loosening. Néron must have left her a loose end when he cut her feet free.

Thanks, guy Scarlett thought as she worked the rope. She slid one hand out but left the rope circled around her right wrist. When you have nothing, a piece of rope could be everything. Scarlett glanced behind her as she headed around the side of the outcrop, but didn't see Brenna following her. For now, anyway. Scarlett kept her back close to one of the rock formations as she came around it, looking carefully for anyone. She realized she was holding her breath and paused for a moment to let it out slowly. Scarlett knew she didn't have much time to make a decision about what to do next, but she also knew it was better to take a breath before rushing into a melee. *Good air in, 2, 3, 4, bad air out, 2, 3, 4. Good air in, 2, 3, 4, bad air out, 2, 3, 4.* She repeated this a few more times until she felt the tension release in her chest. Then it was time to keep moving.

As bullets rang out on the other side of the outcrop, Scarlett continued her slow pace around the perimeter and was rewarded by the sight of several unattended motorbikes. She hurried over and checked them for weapons, but didn't find so much as a knife. *Oh well, naked beggars in a desert can't be choosers.* A bike would at least get her the fuck out of there, something she desperately needed. She grabbed the one closest to her and climbed on. The key was still in the ignition and it purred to life under her touch. Scarlett noticed the red and yellow feathers dangling from one of the handlebars and rolled her eyes.

"Fucking feathers," she muttered.

Just then, the scout wandered out from behind one of the rocks, a little dazed with her hands still secured behind her back. Scarlett knew she should just leave, but something held her there, watching the scout.

"Why would they shoot at me?" the scout asked herself, her voice barely audible to Scarlett. Then the scout lifted her eyes and saw Scarlett. "Why . . ."

"Oh, for fuck's sake, just get on the bike," Scarlett said, tapping her fingers anxiously on the handlebars. She immediately regretted the offer, but for some reason, she felt sorry for this pathetic woman. The scout looked up and her eyes focused on Scarlett, noticing her for the first time.

"Make it right," the scout muttered. "I have to make it right."

Scarlett was now very much regretting her offer.

"I have to make it right," the scout repeated, louder this time. She ran at Scarlett, looking a little ridiculous with her hands still tied behind her back.

"What are you . . ." Scarlett started to ask before the scout slammed into her, knocking her off the bike. Scarlett landed hard on the ground, the scout's full weight on Scarlett's body and the bike's metal, warm from the sun, pressed against her leg.

"Are you fucking kidding me?" Scarlett exclaimed before she shoved the scout off of her. The scout fell easily to the side and rolled away.

"I have to make it right!" the scout screamed at her.

"I don't know what the fuck you're talking about!" Scarlett yelled back at her. *Great idea, genius, make sure everyone knows your location by yelling. What are you, new?*

"I have to explain! I have to get back there! I have to make it right!" the scout shouted.

"Make what right?" Scarlett asked, annoyed. She tried to control the volume of her voice, but this hysterical scout was going to give their location away anyway.

"You! You got away! I have to take you back! If I take you back, I'll make it right! I need my masters to forgive me!" the scout yelled as she climbed back to her feet.

"Your masters?" Scarlett asked, appalled. "Do you even hear yourself? This is your chance to get away from those assholes that beat the hell out of you!"

"DON'T YOU DARE CALL THEM THAT!" the scout screamed as she hurtled herself towards Scarlett. Scarlett sidestepped her easily and stuck out her foot. The scout tripped and fell, landing hard on the cracked desert earth.

"You're fucking crazy, lady," Scarlett said.

The scout groaned and weakly kicked at Scarlett. Scarlett rolled her eyes and went back to the bike, righting it. She climbed on and revved the engine. In the distance, she could see some men advancing on her and the scout's position. Scarlett could tell by their black pants, vests, and shaved heads that they were the same people she'd seen with the scout before she'd entered the mountain pass. She glanced back over at the scout one more time. The scout had risen to her knees but wasn't looking at Scarlett; instead, she was watching the approaching fighters.

"Over here!" the scout shouted, pulling herself up to her feet. The scout ran past Scarlett and sprinted towards the men, her hands still tied behind her back. "Hey! I'm here!"

Scarlett was done. She turned the bike and drove away, heading for the hills in the distance.

"You came back for me!" the scout exclaimed as she drew closer to the Slavers. "You—"

Her words were cut off by a sharp punch to the face. The scout collapsed on the ground, involuntary tears careening down her cheeks.

"Should we go after her?" Hawk asked, pointing to Scarlett.

"She's not worth it," Artem said, running a hand over his bald head.

"But—"

"Don't you see where she's going?" Artem asked, grabbing Hawk's chin and turning his face towards Scarlett. "She's going into the hills. No one survives the beast. She's as good as dead."

15

THE BIKE ROARED between Scarlett's legs as she sped across the desert, kicking up rocks and a storm cloud of dust behind her. She glanced back over her shoulder just in time to see the scout get hit in the face by one of the men. What had Néron called them? Slavers? Whatever, it didn't matter. Scarlett turned back to face the front and she guided the bike around the scrub brush that dotted the landscape. She knew that everyone made their own choices, and if that scout wanted to run back to the men who were most likely going to kill her, that was her decision. Really, it didn't affect Scarlett at all. If anything, the Slavers killing the scout would just mean there was one less person trying to attack her. And yet, Scarlett still felt a nagging tug at the back of her mind at the thought of the scout running back to them, her hands still bound behind her back. Scarlett didn't really give a shit about what people did with their own free will, but what if that scout wasn't actually free?

She's not your concern she scolded herself. *Forget her. She made her choice. You're still naked in a desert, you idiot.*

Scarlett leaned forward, pushing the bike faster towards the hills ahead. So far, she didn't think anyone was following her, but she didn't want to wait to find out. But when she tried to gun the acceleration, the bike began to groan in protest and started to lose speed.

"No, no, no, no," Scarlett protested as the bike slowed, but her pleas fell on the bike's nonexistent, deaf ears. The bike whined as it coasted to a stop before it shut off entirely.

"Are you fucking kidding me?" Scarlett asked. She tried to restart the bike, but to no avail. There wasn't even so much as a click to imply that the bike could start if only she tried hard enough. Scarlett groaned, frustrated, and slowly peeled herself off the bike's seat, her skin slightly sticking to the leather. She glanced back towards the Slavers, but they didn't appear to be heading her way. For now. Scarlett knew she had to hurry before they noticed she'd stopped and wasn't still driving the bike. There wasn't enough time to attempt to repair the bike, so her only option was to try and salvage something useful. There was a canteen attached to the back, which Scarlett grabbed hopefully, but it was empty because of course it was. But this time, she slung the canteen across her body instead of smashing it on the rocks like she'd done with the one Mel had left for her.

Mel. God, it always came back to her, didn't it? *You and I are in serious need of a discussion, Mel* Scarlett thought. *Assuming I ever get out of here and ever manage to find a goddamn shirt.*

Scarlett examined the side of the bike and found a hard plastic panel firmly screwed in place over the gears. She tried to pry it off, but it wouldn't budge. She glanced around for a rock, but then stopped herself. What, was she hoping to find a screwdriver-shaped rock? She could always try to break the panel with a larger rock, something not quite as precise or screwdriver-shaped, but were whatever gears she could hope to find be worth it? Probably not. Scarlett looked back towards the Slavers, and although they didn't seem to have moved closer, a few of them did look like they might be watching her. She quickly surveyed the rest of the bike, but aside from the canteen, she found nothing useful. Scarlett held the red and yellow feathers that hung from the handlebar in her palm of her hand for a moment. Fucking feathers. If she never saw another feather like these, that would be just fine with her.

Scarlett took the rope she'd saved from her captivity and wound it snugly around her left wrist, tucking the ends beneath the coils to secure them. She looked back over at the hills. They were only a quarter of a mile away. Scarlett hated to leave behind a possible means of transportation. Hell, with more time, maybe she could figure out how to get the panel off and fix the bike. But with some of the Slavers already watching her, she knew walking the bike with her would be slower than if she left it behind. She couldn't take the chance of getting close to them again. Scarlett thought of how the scout had looked when she'd found Scarlett at the shack. Beaten within an inch of her life, one eye swollen shut, and her buttocks and the backs of her legs had been shredded to ribbons, most likely by a whip. If that scout was stupid enough to go back to them, that was up to her. As for Scarlett, she wasn't going to give them a chance to catch up. With that thought, Scarlett gave the bike a final once over before she turned and continued on towards the hills.

16

A LOUD CLANGING sound jolted the scout into consciousness. She blinked her eyes, trying to adjust to the gloom of the Slaver underground. Mounted torches lined the walls, flickering eerie shadows across the rows of cages. Where was she? What happened? The last thing she remembered was being in the desert. There had been gunfire, although that wasn't exactly unusual in this area. She'd been reunited with her family, but something wasn't right. Her cheek was sore and the back of her head throbbed. Had one of them hit her? Or had it been one of the Eagles? There had been someone else there, too, but her face was just out of reach of the scout's mind. The scout pushed herself into a sitting position and looked around. Slowly, the cage bars came into focus.

No!

The scout grabbed desperately at the bars when she realized she was on the wrong side. *No, no, no, no, no* she thought frantically as her reality came into focus. She was locked up. She hadn't been locked up in years. That meant . . . oh, god, *no.* The scout suddenly remembered the woman in the desert, the one she'd chased through the mountain pathway. She remembered the beating she'd taken for letting her go, seeing her master's face explode in front of her. The scout looked down at her body and was surprised to see her skin was relatively unmarked. The lashes and scars on the backs of her legs were gone and the once rippled skin felt smooth as glass under her probing fingertips. When had that happened? *How* had that happened? The scout was curious, but there were more pressing issues at hand. There had been a firefight in the desert and that woman had escaped, riding away on a bike. And now . . . The scout slumped against the cage. There was no way to make it right anymore. She had made a mistake, she'd let the woman get away. The scout reached out and gingerly touched one of the bars again. She'd been demoted. Base level. All those years, all that work and service, erased. God, how had she been so stupid? Tears spilled down her cheeks, hot and unwanted over her skin. There had to be something she could do. There had to be a way to fix this.

A pair of legs came to a stop in front of her cage. The scout let her eyes rise until she saw the face of the Slaver standing before her.

"Artem! Sir! Oh thank god," the slave said as she quickly crawled to the other side of the cage. "You saw what happened, you know I went after her. If you can let me out, I can make it right, I can—"

Artem's boot lashed out and kicked the cage, startling the scout and causing her to fall back on her heels as her words fell silent. She let her eyes rise to his face, a hard mask of anger. The light and shadows from the torches twisted across his features. Without looking away from the scout, Artem unzipped his black pants. The scout's muscles tensed, knowing what would come next. She'd seen it before. Hell, she'd experienced it before. There would be a jingle of keys before one slid into the lock, which would open with a clack. She'd be dragged out by her hair, or maybe her arm. Once, she'd been dragged by her foot and the Slaver had left a bracelet of bruises around her ankle. Then she would have to submit, humiliated as the Slaver would do anything he wanted to her in full view of everyone else. Punished, put in her place. The scout knew she deserved it, she'd deserved it every time, but even knowing she deserved it never made it easier.

The scout closed her eyes and braced herself, waiting for the lock to click, her hair to be pulled, her body to be punished, but none of those things ever came. She was shocked when the stream of urine hit her in the face, the smell acrid and thick. The scout didn't move, she didn't dare move, and after a few seconds it was over. She heard the sound of the zipper being pulled once more and she opened her eyes, blinking the foul-smelling liquid away. The scout didn't dare wipe it off her face, not yet. She watched as Artem's boots walked away, but they stopped suddenly, met by two more pairs of boots. The scout discreetly wiped away the urine from her stinging eyes with the back of her hand and shifted her feet out from underneath her, resting her back against the cage bars once more. Without looking at them, she strained her ears to hear what the masters were saying.

". . . keep her alive. For now, anyway."

"What for? We should kill the bitch and make an example of her."

"She spent time in an Eagle camp, she could be useful for once in her miserable fucking life."

"But—"

"The Grand Master said to keep her alive. Do you want to tell him he's wrong? Before you'd even get the words out, The Pet would rip your fucking throat out with her teeth."

The men were silent for a moment. The scout risked a glance up at them and saw one of the Slavers grimace at the thought of The Pet before she averted her eyes again.

"What about that girl?"

"What girl?"

"That cunt that started this whole mess, the one who rode off on that Eagle bike."

"Is she an Eagle?"

"I doubt it. Either way, it doesn't matter. She was riding up the blood path, towards the hills. She won't last ten minutes before the beast rips her in half. Trust me, she's not our problem anymore."

"That's too bad. I could've had some fun with her."

"Yeah, we all could have. But if she means that much to you, you could always follow her into the hills to play with whatever the beast leaves behind."

The three men broke into peals of laughter that echoed throughout the cave.

"No woman is worth that much, one cunt is just like any other."

The scout heard a jingle of keys and allowed herself to raise her eyes again. Artem unlocked a cage two down from where the scout sat. The lock clanged open and he reached inside, pulling up a slave by her arm. The woman stood there weakly, but unprotesting.

"Speaking of," Artem said. "I'll see you fellas later."

The other two Slavers laughed as they and the scout watched as Artem dragged the slave away with him. When Artem and the slave were out of sight, the scout dropped her gaze again.

I have to make them forgive me she thought. *I have to make it right.*

17

Brenna paced back and forth in front of the table in the nearly empty dining hall where Néron sat. Suddenly, Brenna snatched Néron's water glass and threw it against the wall where it smashed, shattering into tiny, jagged fragments.

"Was that necessary?" Néron asked calmly.

"Why the *fuck* did they tell us to stop?" Brenna shouted, her voice echoing slightly in the empty room as her voice ricocheted around them. "We could have taken them!"

"They flanked us," Néron said.

"That's the perfect time, we could have taken them from the inside out," Brenna protested.

"The elders disagreed."

"Oh yeah? Well FUCK—" Brenna shouted before she caught herself at the last moment. "Fuck the . . . fuck that," she corrected.

Néron raised an eyebrow at Brenna, but said nothing.

"It's just . . . you know what it is? It's disrespectful," Brenna said.

"How is it disrespectful to call back troops?" Néron asked. "That's illogical."

"No, it's not!" Brenna argued. "It's very disrespectful, they didn't respect my skills enough to let me take out the Slavers and finish them off."

"That seems like a stretch," Néron said.

Brenna stopped pacing and narrowed her eyes at him.

"Are you questioning your superior?" she asked, her voice quiet but the tension behind it was coiled as tightly as a snake, ready to strike.

Néron said nothing.

"Because I can't imagine that the infallibly correct and honorable Néron would ever do something as disrespectful as questioning his superior," Brenna continued.

Néron's expression remained placid, but his eye contact never wavered. Brenna's gaze broke away first and she turned away, staring at the wall but not really seeing it, her mind's eye filled with wordless fury and gunfire.

Suddenly, both Brenna and Néron heard the sound of running footsteps approaching. They turned their heads in unison towards the entrance to the dining hall and in ran a scout, breathless and panting.

"What is it, any news?" Brenna asked impatiently. The scout attempted to steady his breathing enough to speak.

"The elders are requesting a council with you and the other captains to determine a strategy against the Slavers. Immediately."

Brenna rolled her eyes.

"And what about that woman, any sign of her?"

The scout shook his head and swallowed some air.

"No, nothing. She went into the blood hills."

Brenna was still for a moment, glaring at the scout, before she suddenly turned and grabbed the edge of a nearby table, flipping it onto its side.

"You need to calm down," Néron said evenly.

"Calm down?" Brenna shouted. "Calm down? She robbed me! That fucking bitch robbed me! And then I was finally in a position to kill those Slavers, but then I'm told to fall back and wait for reinforcements! Don't fucking tell me to calm down!"

The scout said nothing, his eyes wide with surprise.

"Look, the elders said to fall back, so you fell back. End of story," Néron said. "I'm sure they had a good reason. It's not like you're never going to get to kill Slavers, they want you for a strategy meeting to discuss what comes next."

"Right. Discuss," Brenna muttered.

"As for the girl . . . if it's true that she went into the hills, then she's not going to be a problem anymore."

"So she just gets away with stealing?" Brenna demanded.

"I hardly consider the fate of the hills to be 'getting away' with anything," Néron replied.

"You know, this wouldn't have been an issue if *someone* hadn't let her go," Brenna said, her eyes sharp and narrow as she glared at Néron.

"I didn't let her go, I just didn't leave her to be a sitting duck to be murdered—or worse—by Slavers," Néron said.

"Right, your honor code," Brenna said, rolling her eyes again.

"Yes, *our* honor code," Néron countered.

"I'm sorry to interrupt, but the elders have requested you go to their chambers immediately," the scout said.

"Yeah, yeah, I'm going," Brenna said, turning to leave the dining hall.

Néron stood to follow.

"I hope that beast rips her to pieces," Brenna muttered.

18

THE SUN WAS setting in the hills and Scarlett knew she had to find shelter. She had escaped the firefight, but God only knew what was lurking in the hills. *I swear to God, if I find yet another tribe of people trying to murder me in here, I'm going to completely lose my shit.* The path into the hills was rocky and Scarlett found herself wishing yet again for a pair of boots. She was fairly certain no one from the firefight was chasing her, so she was able to walk slowly. However, as the sky darkened, her steps were getting more careless and her feet were beginning to ache. God, what she would've given for at least a pair of socks right now. The area within the hills was far more lush than Scarlett had expected, with trees and grassy areas that were a patchwork of green and sun bleached vegetation. There had to be some sort of water source in here to explain this little desert oasis, Scarlett just knew it. It couldn't come too soon either. Scarlett's throat felt dry and she found herself increasingly desperate for a drink of water.

Remember, idiot she told herself. *This time, don't bleed in your water source.*

As twilight began to settle over the valleys nestled in the hills, the landscape around her began to rustle with life. Tree branches swayed slightly as birds stopped and started from between their leaves. The ground whispered as creatures crawled and slithered across it. Scarlett's uneven footsteps felt brazen and intrusive amidst this serene haven.

Sorry, everybody Scarlett thought. *I don't mean to just barge in like this, but it's either invite myself in, or stay out there with those crazy fucks.*

As the sun continued to descend, the temperature dropped and Scarlett felt goosebumps ripple across her exposed flesh. Alright, it was decision time. She didn't have a light source and she didn't think the moon would be enough to illuminate her path. She had to pick a spot for the night, it was her only choice. She'd hoped to find the water before doing so, but if she couldn't, then that was that. Scarlett would admit that she'd made some stupid choices throughout her life, but stumbling around unfamiliar terrain in the dark without so much as a pair of pants was not one she was eager to add to the list.

Up ahead to her left, Scarlett saw a ravine. She walked towards it, her feet tender and complaining with every step. She leaned over the edge a little, but couldn't see the bottom in the darkening light. Scarlett listened intently as a small desert breeze ruffled her hair. She wasn't sure if it was real or a desperate conjuring of her imagination, but Scarlett could swear she heard the sound of running water. Maybe she'd get a chance to quench her thirst after all. She quickly surveyed the area, hoping for some kind of path down into the ravine, but found none. Scarlett figured there was probably one somewhere, but there was no time to look. She did, however, see pieces of rock and tree roots sticking out of the ravine walls. *That will have to do, I guess.* Scarlett knelt down and slowly lowered her legs over the side, her toes finding purchase on the smallest of ledges. *Here goes nothing.*

Scarlett took the route slowly, feeling her way down along the wall. Her toes grew weak during the descent, and several times they slipped off whatever small hold they had. Scarlett dug her fingers into the smallest hold, using every ounce of strength to keep her fingertips from slipping as well. She'd never attempted something quite like this without at least a rope. Technically, Scarlett supposed she had a rope, but it was still coiled around her left wrist. No way that short of a rope could even hope to be useful during this climb. The same went for the canteen strap. Her hands were sweaty, but her bare skin wasn't much of a towel. Scarlett rubbed her hand against the rock wall, rough and unyielding beneath her touch, desperate to pick up any kind of dirt that could dry out some of the moisture. *I will not fall, god dammit* she told herself. *I can't survive all that bullshit out there just to die because I had some great idea about finding water at the bottom of a fucking ravine that I can't even see in because the goddamn sun is going down.* Scarlett did her best to control her breathing. *Good air in, 2, 3, 4, bad air out, 2, 3, 4. Good air in, 2, 3, 4, bad air out, 2, 3, 4. Do. Not. Panic.*

Scarlett took her right foot and stretched it down carefully, feeling for some kind of ledge. Instead, her toes swiped at soft earth. Relieved, Scarlett jumped off the wall, her heels sinking into the mud. She crouched down, leaning her back against the rock wall. Scarlett placed her hands flat on the ground, the cool soil a welcome antidote to her burning fingers.

"Never again," Scarlett said aloud, her strained breathing starting to return to its normal rhythm. There was very little light down at the bottom of the ravine, but her eyes began to adjust and she could still make out some shapes. Splayed out in front of her was a sizeable pile of oddly shaped rocks with lots of sharp edges. Scarlett was grateful she'd managed to hold on to the rock wall during her descent; falling on that particular pile seemed like a rather unpleasant way to end an adventure.

One of the rocks had fallen off the pile and was sitting near Scarlett's foot. She leaned forward to examine it and tugged, releasing it from its muddy hold. Scarlett squinted as she ran her fingers over the surface. Then, she recognized it. In her hand, Scarlett held a human skull. She let her eyes drift over to the other rocks and she realized that they weren't rocks at all. Before her lay a pile of bones, picked clean by an animal. Or animals. The pile reminded her of a tavern she and Mel used to go to. A rougher crowd ran through that joint, and diners often tossed the remains of their turkey legs into a pile in the center of the room, a shrine to dominance over prey and the prosperity of a fully belly. Mel had been disgusted by it, but Scarlett had found it amusing. Now, the memory made her stomach roil in revulsion.

"Oh, fuck."

19

THE ELDER CAVE was a cacophonous disaster, each Eagle captain shouting louder than the last. The seven elders sat stoically at one end of the room, silently regarding the commotion. The High Elder, seated in the middle, looked vaguely amused, a smile tugging at the corners of her mouth. One by one, the captains began to notice the elders watching them and they fell silent as well.

"If you're finished, we'd like to discuss the strategy for the Slavers," the High Elder finally said.

The captains said nothing, chastised, and awaited further instruction.

"The council and I have discussed it, and we believe it would be best to attack one of their outlying camps." The High Elder nodded to two attendants who brought out a large map of the area. The High Elder stood up and circled to the front of the map, facing the captains. "There," she said, pointing.

"That's awfully close to their home base," one of the captains said.

"This is true," the High Elder said. "But after careful discussion, we would rather take the fight to them instead of wait for them to come to us."

"And give them homefield advantage?" Brenna asked.

The High Elder tilted her head slightly, examining Brenna.

"Are you questioning your superior?" the High Elder asked.

"No," Brenna said quietly.

The High Elder watched her for another moment.

"Where would you suggest we fight the Slavers?" she asked.

"Well . . . where we matched them today was an excellent spot. We were in a position to take them out before we were pulled back," Brenna said.

"You were flanked, and you would have lost," the High Elder said.

"No, we weren't, we—" Brenna argued.

"You would have lost," the High Elder repeated, her voice louder this time. The other captains were so silent that the sound of their breathing could scarcely be heard. "Besides, I hear your attention was . . . elsewhere."

Brenna's face flushed red.

"I had good cause," Brenna said.

"Better than defending your people?"

"There was a thief," Brenna said. "We captured her, but she got away."

"And what did she steal?" the High Elder asked. Her amused smile had returned to her lips, but her eyes were steely and fixed on Brenna.

"She stole . . . an item of value. From me," Brenna said carefully.

"Ah," said the High Elder. "I see. Based on your reluctance to divulge the nature of this stolen item, I am left to infer that it is something that you yourself should not have been in possession of to begin with. Is that correct?"

Brenna dropped her gaze to the floor, her face and ears redder than ever. The other captains averted their eyes, too embarrassed to look at her.

"I suggest, Captain," the High Elder said, "that you drop this petty grievance and focus on the task at hand. Behave with the honor befitting your rank, else the council should be forced to . . . reconsider your position."

Brenna swallowed hard, the blood thrumming in her ears.

"That reminds me," the High Elder continued as she took slow, measured steps towards Brenna. "Someone was recently spotted near the elder chambers and a few items went missing. Once this matter with the Slavers has been resolved, I would like to discuss adding extra security." She stopped in front of Brenna and reached out a long finger, tilting Brenna's face up to hers. "You'll remind me, won't you, Captain?"

Angry tears spilled from Brenna's eyes as she refused to meet the High Elder's gaze.

"Thank you," the High Elder said. "I appreciate that I can count on you to honor my request."

The High Elder released Brenna's chin and walked back to the front of the room to stand beside the map.

"If there are no other questions, I'd like to proceed with our strategy," the High Elder said.

As she continued, the captains kept their eyes riveted on the High Elder, doing their best to memorize each word that came from her mouth. The smallest detail could mean the difference between life and death for their troops. One captain, however, heard nothing, save for the beating of her own heart as it thundered in her ears, her hands clenched into fists that made her palms ache.

20

SCARLETT'S HEART HAMMERED in her chest and she had to use all of her focus to gently set down the skull in front of her. Whatever creature had done this clearly returned to this spot often, and Scarlett didn't want to give away her position. If she hadn't already. Fuck. With every second that passed, Scarlett regretted climbing down into the ravine more and more. She should've just found a safe spot and burrowed there for the night. But would it have mattered? With a beast like this running around and devouring humans, she likely would've been picked off while she slept. At least now she still had a chance of survival. Well, as big of a chance as a person could have after they wandered into a predator's dining room.

As the sun fully set, the moon offered more light than Scarlett had expected. It was nearly full, a swollen belly hanging high above her. Her vision wasn't great in the moonlight, but it was better than total darkness. God, what if there had been a new moon? If she thought she was fucked now, she really would've been fucked then. *Stop thinking about how bad it could have been* she scolded herself. *It's not like now is all that great either. Focus!*

Scarlett took a deep breath. Think. She had to think. Okay, if there was a big creature that tossed its leftovers here, there had to be some way to get down into the ravine that didn't involve scaling the wall. There had to be some kind of pathway out. Scarlett looked left, then right. God, neither one of them looked promising. She had a feeling that this creature probably lived in, or at least near, the ravine. The last thing she wanted to do was wander into its den because Jesus Christ, hadn't she done enough of that over the last couple days? If it wasn't the Slavers, it was the fucking feather people, and now all Scarlett figured she needed to do in order to complete the trifecta was stroll into some beast's den. Although, really, after dealing with both of those tribes over the last couple days, Scarlett was pretty sure she'd prefer to take on the beast. Then again, she thought that now without having actually seen the beast. She's heard stories about weird creatures in various parts of the country. A lot of people said they were due to some of the chemicals and radiations people used to use on their crops, back before the world collapsed into its current state. Rather than just kill the animals, the chemicals did weird things to the animals' DNA and warped them into something else entirely. Scarlett tried to remember what kind of animals she'd heard lived in the deserts, but the fearful adrenaline from finding the skull was still pumping through her body and clouding her mind. She vaguely remembered hearing something about a rabbit with horns . . . what was that called? A jackalope? Yes, that seemed right. Scarlett shook her head. Even if she did accept the stories about strange animals, that one seemed a little too much like bullshit to believe. And anyway, a rabbit, even a rabbit with horns, wouldn't be able to take down humans and pick their bones clean.

Right?

Scarlett turned left and started to carefully make her way through the ravine, away from the pile of bones. The earth was soft and she felt her feet sink into the damp soil with each step, but it couldn't be helped —she couldn't see well enough to find something else to step on and avoid leaving footprints. Scarlett rolled her eyes as she thought again about how if one were to judge her survival skills based on the last couple days, no one would ever hire her for another job again. Leaving a trail of bloody footprints to the shack, bleeding into a clean water source, letting herself get captured by the feather people, nearly getting shot by Slavers, and now she'd wandered into some beast's lair and was leaving a clearly defined trail for it to follow and eat her. Christ, she wouldn't hire herself either.

As she walked, the ground slowly began to rise in an incline beneath her feet, gently leading her upwards and out of the ravine. Scarlett was glad she wouldn't be left to scale the wall again, but felt annoyed she hadn't found this way before. However, there was no time to focus on what she could've done in light of what she needed to do and needed to find. Water. Scarlett knew she needed to find water. Yes, she was thirsty, but if she could find a pond or a river, she could cut off her scent trail. She had no idea if this creature was nocturnal or how many of them there were, so she was going to need every tactical advantage she could get. Unfortunately, Scarlett could feel the ground drying beneath her feet the further she rose out of the ravine, so she wasn't sure how probable her plan of finding water was going to be without descending back into the ravine. She took the final steps out of the ravine and looked around at the scenery, bathed in moonlight. A slow breeze meandered through the hills, gently rustling the leaves of the trees. Scarlett glanced over her shoulder, unsure of what she expected to see, but found nothing save for the gentle sway of the oasis greenery. She turned back around and headed into the trees that lined the ravine, moving as quietly as possible.

21

THE SLAVER BIKES and trucks swarmed like angry wasps as they approached their outlier camp. Grun led his hoard on his bike with The Pet sitting alert in the sidecar. Grun liked the feel of the bike underneath him, the rumble of its engine made him feel powerful. He was looking forward to the fight with the Eagles. Grun glanced over his shoulder at the trucks behind him. Their cages were empty now, but he looked forward to filling them with new slaves as his spoils of war. Of course, it would be years before any of them could even hope to be anywhere near The Pet's level, but Grun figured he could use some more toys.

Grun could see what looked like the camp master waiting in front of the encampment with several men beside him. Good. Evidently, they remembered what happened the last time Grun arrived and there hadn't been anyone to greet them. Well, Grun was sure that at least Caro remembered. After all, that was how he'd been given the opportunity to take over from his forgetful predecessor.

Grun pulled his bike to a stop and swung his leg over so he was standing beside it. Caro and the other

Slavers immediately dropped to one knee, bowing their heads. Grun sniffed as he surveyed them. Some of the bowing men were in need of a shave, their hair was beginning to grow in like shadows across their scalps. Grun considered making an example of them, but he knew it wasn't a good idea to incapacitate any of his men with an impending war. Oh well. There was, however, someone of whom he could make an example.

"Where is she?" Grun asked.

Caro stood up and motioned for his men to do the same.

"Inside. We have her locked up on the lower level," Caro said, looking past Grun. "Is that all we have for reinforcements?" he asked, sounding a little worried. "We received intel that the Eagles are planning on attacking here, and we need to be sure we have enough men to hold them off."

Grun stared at him for a moment. When Caro's eyes cautiously flicked back to Grun's, Grun raised his arm and backhanded Caro across the face, knocking him into the dirt. Caro landed hard with a grunt on all fours. Grun glanced up at Caro's men, daring one of them to move, but none of them did. Instead, they stood silently, their eyes fixed forward, stiller than statues.

"What do you take me for, a fool?" Grun asked, his voice saccharine and dangerous. The Pet turned her head towards her master, her gun already drawn and pointed at Caro. Grun shook his head and waved her off. The Pet lowered her gun and her shoulders slackened a little. She was disappointed. Grun smiled at the sight. Soon enough, she would get what she wanted. But right now, she had to be a good dog and wait.

"Well, do you?" Grun asked again, his voice terrifyingly light.

"No, sir," Caro said quietly before he spit blood into the dirt between his hands.

"I didn't think so," Grun said, his voice returning to its normal cadence. "Each camp is sending troops and they should be arriving shortly." Grun stared at Caro for a moment before lashing out his boot, connecting the steel toed shoe with Caro's ribs. Caro grunted again and fell on his side in the dirt. Grun enjoyed the sight, a man quivering in the dirt before him, brought down by Grun's own power. He rather liked that feeling. He would've enjoyed keeping it for a while longer, but there were things to do. Such is life.

"If you're done wasting my time with your questions, I have some business to attend to," Grun said. "Take me to her."

Caro shakily climbed to his feet.

"Need a hand?" Grun asked innocently.

"No, sir," Caro said. "Thank you."

"Start setting up," Grun instructed The Pet. She nodded immediately. "Take her to the arena," Grun said to Caro's men. "Clear it out and assist her with whatever she needs."

Caro's men nodded, but they eyed The Pet warily.

"Now," Grun said, turning back to Caro. "Let's go."

Caro led all of them inside the encampment down a pathway until it diverged into a fork. Caro led Grun to the left and The Pet headed right with Caro's men. She walked behind them, one hand always on her gun. Just in case. Grun caught a couple of the men glancing over their shoulders at The Pet, their expressions seemingly wishing to find her vanished rather than at their heels. But there she was, doing her duty. The men turned back and headed to the arena to do theirs. Grun didn't like to be apart from The Pet, but he didn't want anyone else to know that. The slightest chink in the armor could be disastrous.

Caro and Grun walked towards a squat building where there were two low-level slaves waiting beside the doors. The two women sprang into action and pulled open the doors for Grun and Caro, bowing their heads as they did so. Grun breezed by them without acknowledgment. Caro led him down the hall and to a set of stairs where the two men descended deeper and deeper until they found themselves down in a dimly lit room, lined with four rows of cages. Caro paused to confer briefly with one of the Slavers who pointed down the first row. Caro turned back to Grun.

"This way, sir," Caro said.

Grun followed Caro about halfway down the line before they came to a stop in front of one cage, a slave curled on her side on the floor, her eyes closed. Caro kicked the cage and the slave sprang up, her eyes wide and terrified.

"This is her?" Grun asked, leaning in slightly to examine the woman.

"Yes," Caro confirmed.

Grun sniffed, the acrid smell of stale, dehydrated urine making his nose wrinkle.

"Christ, she stinks like the Eagles," Grun muttered. He squinted in the dim light. "Alright, get her cleaned up. We're going to do this from scratch."

With that, Grun turned on his heel and walked away. Caro signaled to one of the other Slavers and held a brief conversation with him that the scout couldn't hear. She watched Grun's receding back as he left, his footsteps fading away. Caro soon followed him. The other Slaver pulled a ring of keys from his pocket and snapped open the lock on the scout's cage.

"Let's go," he said.

The scout stood up obediently, doing her best to hide her trembling hands.

22

THE SCOUT FOLLOWED the Slaver out of the cage room and up the stairs. She wasn't shackled, but she knew that was because restraints were an unnecessary precaution to use on her. They knew she wasn't going to run and if she did, she wouldn't be able to run far before someone put a bullet in her head—or worse. Not that the scout wanted to run away. Why would she leave her family? Of course, they weren't pleased with her at the moment, but that was only temporary. The scout was sure of it. Soon, she'd be able to make it right, get back to the way things used to be.

Once upstairs, she followed the Slaver down a long hallway to a room with a faded green door. The Slaver banged on the door twice, the sound jarring the quiet hall and making the scout jump slightly. The Slaver noticed her involuntary movement and glared at her for a moment before turning his attention back to the door. It swung open to reveal a blonde slave, her hair tied back tightly in a ponytail. The scout watched as the slave kept her eyes fixed down towards the ground, carefully folding her hands in front of her.

"Get her ready, back to base zero," the Slaver said, pointing to the scout. The slave let her eyes rise enough to examine the scout, taking in her dirt stained limbs and foul smell. The slave nodded. The Slaver grabbed the scout's arm and practically threw her into the slave, who had to catch the scout to keep them both from tumbling to the ground. The slave led the scout inside the room and the Slaver slammed the door shut behind them. As he did so, the overhead light flickered on, giving the room a sallow glow. Base zero? What was base zero? The scout tried to remember, but nothing came to her. There were two other slaves in the room and once the door clicked shut, they got to work. There was a sink in the corner along with a large bucket and an assortment of scrubbers, soaps, and various bottles of . . . well, the scout wasn't really sure what they were. The blonde slave who had answered the door led the scout to the middle of the room and positioned her over a drain in the floor. Then, the slave removed the scout's vest and motioned for the scout to hand over her boots. The scout did as the slave silently requested and the slave carefully set them aside on a bench by the door.

Meanwhile, the other two slaves filled a black plastic bucket with water from the sink. They brought the bucket over to the scout and unceremoniously dumped it over her head. The scout sputtered, but didn't protest. The water was a comfortable temperature and the scout couldn't remember the last time she'd really bathed. The scout waited patiently in the middle of the room as one of the slaves refilled the bucket. Then, all three of the slaves began to scrub the scout, their gentle, circular motions washing away the desert from her body. The bubbles on the scout's skin had a slight scent of something warm and sweet, although the scout couldn't place it. It was unlike anything she usually smelled, save for some of the cactus blooms. But even then, this wasn't quite the same. The scent softened the scout a little, letting her relax for a moment. Maybe "get her cleaned up" and "starting from scratch" were good things. Maybe this was a fresh start for her with the family. Maybe everything would be okay.

One of the slaves refilled the bucket with fresh water and slowly tipped the contents over the scout's head. She raised her face towards the light above her and felt a sense of rebirth as the water rivulets ran down her legs. This could be her fresh start. This could be good. This could be great. One of the slaves began to massage the scout's hair with a thick cream that smelled even stronger of that warm, sweet scent. The scout closed her eyes as she felt the slave's fingers work through her hair, a blissful calm radiating out from her scalp that tingled down her spine.

When the slave stopped washing the scout's hair, the scout briefly opened her eyes as she waited for one of the other slaves to refill the water bucket. It was then that the scout noticed The Pet. The scout wasn't sure when The Pet had come into the room—she was almost certain The Pet hadn't been there before. Then again, the scout couldn't have sworn it for certain one way or the other. The Pet leaned casually in one corner of the room, a stance that was almost more disarming than any other detail about her. The Pet was normally so rigid as she stood at attention. It was hard to picture her resting, although the scout was sure The Pet had to at some point. Still, it was difficult to fathom someone who stood as ramrod straight as The Pet doing anything so relaxed as sleeping. And yet, here she was, leaning in the corner. Her feet were crossed lightly, one scuffed black boot over the other, and her helmeted head rested against the tiled wall. The scout's pulse began to pick up speed as she took in the sight of The Pet and let her eyes drift down to The Pet's hands. The Pet held a knife, turning it over in her hands as she faced the scout. She ran a calloused finger over the flat side of the knife before tapping it lightly against the tip of the blade. Although The Pet stood in shadow, the knife glinted and flashed whenever it caught the light. The scout felt a deep sinking feeling in her belly, one that pulled at her muscles, and her heartbeat pounded wildly in her ears. How could she have been so stupid? Of course this wasn't a good thing. The Pet didn't do anything without express permission from the Grand Master. If The Pet was here, she was here on his orders.

Water splashed down over the scout's head, but this time she didn't close her eyes. The shampoo bubbles stung, but she could still make out The Pet through the watery curtain. The scout didn't know why she was being pampered, but the presence of The Pet could only be an omen of one thing: death.

23

GRUN SAT BACK in his chair in the camp's inner sanctum, borrowed from Caro. "Borrowed" was probably too generous of a word, considering Grun hadn't asked. Not that he gave a shit, but sometimes semantics were important. Such was the case with the semantics of the scout. Grun propped his feet up on the desk, knocking loose small sprays of dust from his boots. He didn't necessarily care for the politics of his position, but Grun knew they were essential to maintaining his power. He'd been looking for an excuse to take on the Eagles for a long time. God, he hated them, the Eagles and their fucking honor code. The only way to rule was by brute strength—and by out stepping everyone around you.

Even with the excuse of Kip's half-blown off face on a spike—and Grun knew it was a tepid excuse at best—pulling off a war against the Eagles was going to be difficult. There was a reason the Slavers didn't often venture into Eagle territory. The last time war had been attempted, the Slavers had lost a huge number of their own. Grun remembered that day, nearly a decade earlier. The desert had been strewn with Slavers and slaves alike, their bodies broken and still as their blood seeped into the thirsty desert earth. Grun had only been a general then. His bike had been shot to hell and his arm had been bleeding profusely. He'd stopped over the body of a Slaver, the man's face shot clean off. Grun had pulled his knife from his belt and cut off some of the fabric from the dead man's pants, wrapping the black strip around his arm to try to stifle the bleeding. Grun had pulled it tight, the fabric biting against the open wound, and stuck the knife back in his belt. He'd scanned the scattered bodies, looking for some kind of life. And then he'd seen him. Riker, the Grand Master, lying on the ground. Grun had watched him for a moment, the bone protruding grotesquely from Riker's leg. After about a minute or two, Riker had looked over and caught Grun staring at him.

"Grun," Riker had croaked. "Get over here. I need help."

Grun had walked to him and stood over the Grand Master. Grun had always thought of Riker as a large, imposing man. Intimidating. Frightening, even. But seeing him on the ground, reduced to this raw pain . . . he had just looked small and pathetic.

"What are you waiting for?" Riker had asked, annoyed. "Let's go."

Grun had looked at him for another moment. Then he'd knelt down, pulled his knife free from his belt, and cut Riker's throat. The man's eyes had gogged in surprised and he'd tried to speak, but his words had been lost in a choking of blood that bubbled over the knife. Riker's hand had clawed weakly and ineffectively at Grun's bended knee before falling to the dirt, still for the final time. Grun had stared at Riker's lifeless, unseeing eyes, still open and gazing in astonishment, for a long time. Finally, Grun had wiped the slowly coagulating blood on the blade off on his pants and stood up again. It was done.

Years later, Grun found himself wishing for a simpler situation. Back then, he'd seen something he'd wanted and he'd taken it. Simple as that. But now . . . he couldn't be sure, but he suspected there was dissent among some of the Slavers. He wasn't sure if he was just being paranoid or if he was viewing the situation accurately, but he couldn't be too careful. This war with the Eagles was going to solidify things one way or another. If they won, Grun's authority would be unquestioned. But if they lost . . . well, that was an option he didn't want to consider. Everyone feared The Pet, and hers was the one loyalty Grun never questioned. But if the whole compound revolted against him, The Pet could only hold them off for so long. Longer than most, to be sure, but the ending would be inevitable.

Unless . . . unless he had a backup plan. It was a slim one, but it was all he had at the moment. That stupid bitch, the one that had been in the Eagle camp. He'd planned on killing her, but maybe he could delay that for a bit. He could torture her for information now, make an example of her, but keep her alive for the time being. If the war went Grun's way, he could kill that scout and be done with her. If it didn't, perhaps he could divert the blame to her. She was the one who disobeyed orders, she's the one who fired into Eagle territory, she's the one who got that halfwit Kip's head blown off. If the Slavers lost, he could throw the scout to them, let them tear her to pieces with their bare hands. After a loss, they'd be angry and want blood. Hers would be perfect. Or, if not perfect, at least preferable to his.

There was an assertive knock on the door. Two raps, not the usual three. Thank god it was her.

"Come in," Grun said.

The Pet opened the door and stepped inside, awaiting further instructions.

"Is she ready?" Grun asked.

The Pet nodded curtly. Grun pulled his boots off the desk and dropped his feet heavily to the floor. He straightened up to his full height. Never a shudder, never a chink in the armor. Not even in front of her.

"Let's go," Grun said. The Pet nodded and waited for him by the door. Grun paused only to pull a particularly evil looking bullwhip off a hook on the wall. He smiled.

24

SCARLETT SHIFTED UNCOMFORTABLY in the tree, the bark scratching and digging into her bare skin. Her muscles ached and exhaustion permeated every cell in her body. She'd found the tree hours ago and had climbed up, choosing a resting spot high enough to where she figured if something climbed the tree, it'd shake her awake. Not that she'd really been able to sleep anyway. She'd gotten lucky enough to find two branches that formed a nice crook in which she could rest, but paranoia of falling out of the tree and breaking her neck kept her from succumbing to anything more substantial than a light doze. If the rope twined around her wrist had been longer, she could've used it to tie her waist to the tree and allowed herself more rest, but it was simply too short. And she'd certainly tried, straining the rope around the trunk and each possible branch, but it was just shy of useful. She supposed she could've tied her hands or feet to the tree as some sort of safety leash, but Scarlett felt certain she'd fall out of the tree and dislocate her shoulder. She was already naked, cold, and a strong candidate to become the dinner of a prolific predator; she didn't need to create more problems for herself.

Several times throughout the night, Scarlett had seen a large creature lumbering beneath the tree in the darkness. Even with the strong moonlight, she'd been unable to make out what it was. The bulk of its shape looked like a bear, but its movements were feline and it had a cat-like tail that stretched behind it. It was far too large to be a mountain lion, but bears didn't have tails like that. At least, the bears Scarlett knew of didn't. To be fair, Scarlett supposed, it wasn't like she was familiar with every sort of bear in the world. In actuality, she'd only ever seen a couple in her life and even then, it had been from a distance. Scarlett hadn't bothered them, and they hadn't bothered her. This creature, however, was different. On more than one pass, Scarlett had seen the moon reflect off the beast's eyes like twin shards of glass when it paused beneath the tree, looking up at her. It didn't appear to be motivated enough to want to climb up the tree to get her, which felt lucky. Or perhaps it knew better than to exhaust its energy to climb the tree, knowing Scarlett would eventually have to come down. Although she couldn't swear it, she felt fairly certain it was the same beast that passed beneath her over and over again, rather than multiple different creatures, all equally huge and with similar staring problems.

Scarlett shifted again in the tree, attempting in vain to find a more comfortable way to sit. The skin on her backside felt raw and sharp after so many hours in the same spot. She hadn't expected to miss that stupid shack with its missing door, but at least there hadn't been a predatory creature stalking her.

Hadn't there been, though? Scarlett asked herself. She supposed that scout could have counted as a predatory creature. When animals hunted, they were working off instinct. It wasn't personal, they weren't hunting you with a personal vendetta because you'd inadvertently stolen some fancy medicinal cream from them. Instead, it was programmed into their brains. They were hungry, you were food. Simple as that. The scout was a person, but her brainwashing seemed so evident to Scarlett, especially once she'd watched her eagerly run back to those Slavers. Scarlett wondered what had happened to the scout once she'd gone back to them. They hadn't shot her immediately, so maybe there was hope for her yet. Ordinarily, Scarlett would've shaken thoughts like that from her head, but there was little else to do in the tree at the moment. The only other thoughts that pushed at her mind were ones of Mel, and Scarlett didn't particularly want to think about Mel right then.

"God dammit, Mel," Scarlett muttered, her voice sounding unusual and foreign in the quiet night air. Really, what sort of conniving bitch dropped a person in a desert full of sadistic Slavers and insane feather people? Scarlett thought again of the scout. Sure, that bitch was crazy, but maybe it wasn't her fault. And yeah, she'd tried to kill Scarlett on a couple different occasions, but maybe she wasn't unlike the creature down on the ground. Maybe it was just the way her brain was programmed to work.

Scarlett leaned back in the crook of branches, wishing desperately for some rest, some real relaxation to recharge her body. She didn't even care about getting a full night's sleep. Hell, she couldn't even remember the last time she'd really slept well. She and Mel and the team had usually been on the move and had never stayed anywhere for longer than had been necessary to complete a job. Mercenaries weren't exactly popular amongst locals, and they'd found it best to keep moving. But at least in the group, they could take turns sleeping if they were in a rough area, letting some of them rest while others stood guard, guns at the ready to ward off any predators, animal or otherwise. Now, Scarlett was treed like a naked mole rat and totally alone. She wished she had been able to hang on to that last can of beans from the shack. Her stomach grumbled in agreement, so she reached over and peeled off another piece of bark, chewing on one end like a dog with a bone. Working her jaw usually tricked her stomach into feeling satisfied for at least a little bit, but Scarlett felt like perhaps she'd drawn from that well too many times. Her stomach appeared to be onto her deception and growled in protest.

"Shh!" she admonished her stomach. Christ, even her bodily functions were conspiring against her to give away her position. Sure, the creature had already figured it out, but who knew what else was out there? Scarlett sure as hell didn't. She closed her eyes and pictured herself sitting in a tavern, a hot plate of food sitting before her, steam still rising off the meat, newly pulled off the spit for her. Beside it, a cold beer, the thick froth a precursor on her tongue before the hops fizzed in her mouth. Her stomach growled again.

"Shh!" she insisted again, opening her eyes once more. That was when her gaze met the wide eyes beside her in the tree, staring straight back at her.

25

Scarlett shrieked and felt herself start to slip. Her arms darted out wildly and clawed the branches, her feet locking around the tree. Scarlett felt the bark grind under her fingertips and between her legs, but she held on tightly until she was sure she was no longer moving. The owl beside her appeared bored and gave her a baleful, irritated look before it spread its wings and flew over to a nearby tree. Scarlett was fairly certain she'd never inconvenienced an owl before, but apparently the past few days had been full of firsts. The adrenaline coursing through her body mixed with her empty stomach made her feel slightly nauseated, but Scarlett did her best to stay calm and not further dehydrate herself by vomiting. *Good air in, 2, 3, 4, bad air out, 2, 3, 4. Good air in, 2, 3, 4, bad air out, 2, 3, 4.* She still felt a little sick, but she felt better, and at that point, better was an outcome she was happy to accept. Christ, she had to get out of this goddamn tree. Plus, it didn't help that she was fairly certain she'd just made a rather loud shrieking noise. If the beast hadn't been completely sure where she was, it had to know for sure now. God, the carelessness with which she'd been conducting herself over the past few days blew her fucking mind that anyone had ever hired her to do a job. No, she knew she couldn't think like that. She was good at her job, damn good at her job, and that was the only reason she was still alive at this point. Sure, she'd made some mistakes, but she was human. Not that Scarlett ever enjoyed admitting the weakness of her humanity to anyone, but it existed whether she acknowledged it or not. Like the sun rising each morning, or that scout's intense determination to capture and/or kill Scarlett; some things were just a given.

Maybe she just had to change the way she was viewing the situation. Instead of looking at it like some survivalist experiment, maybe she needed to think of this like a job. A job that went horribly awry, but a job nonetheless. Scarlett had never failed a job before, and she didn't intend to start now. What's the first thing she'd do if this were a job and she found herself in a predicament with no clothes and no weapons? Easy: she'd find clothes and weapons. The clothing still seemed unlikely, but perhaps the weapons weren't. She was finally around some living trees instead of just lying beside a dead one and a huge boulder. One of the branches could at least be made into a crude spear. She could make something a little more refined with a knife, but if she had a knife she probably wouldn't need the spear.

Oh my god, would you fucking focus? Scarlett scolded herself. Then a thought occurred to her. Back down in the ravine, amongst all the bones, what if there were weapons? Surely, most people who came in here were armed with something. It wasn't like the creature was going to have much use for a knife or a rifle. If it did, Scarlett was in much deeper shit than she'd anticipated, but it would be best to cross that bridge when she came to it.

Scarlett knew she had to wait until the creature passed under the tree again before she could climb down. She couldn't remember which way it had been walking the last time she saw it. It's not like she had a lot going on in the tree, so, in theory, she knew she should be able to remember. But the encounter with the owl and pure exhaustion made her memory a little fuzzy. She'd have to wait. Scarlett shifted in the tree, trying to get comfortable, which turned out to be an exercise in futility. She sighed heavily, resigned to the unpleasant makeshift seat under her tailbone, and waited.

Hours later, when the sky finally began to lighten, the beast finally reappeared beneath Scarlett. It ambled slowly from the direction Scarlett had come and she felt relieved to see it was walking away from the ravine, not towards it. When the beast was directly beneath her, it stopped and stared up through the branches at Scarlett, its eyes wide and dark. Scarlett stayed as still as she could as she met the gaze of the creature. They looked at each other for a long time before the creature put a massive paw on the tree, pulling itself up to stand on its back legs. Although she was out of range of the creature, Scarlett slowly pulled her feet a little higher. Just in case. The animal stared at her, their eyes locked. Several moments passed. Finally, the animal slowly lowered its front paws back down to the ground, never once breaking eye contact. It watched Scarlett for a long time before it finally turned and walked away.

Scarlett exhaled slowly, unaware that she'd been holding her breath. She waited until the creature's footsteps faded into the distance. Then, step by step, Scarlett slowly climbed down. When her feet touched the ground, she squinted her eyes in the direction the creature had gone, searching for any sign of it. Nothing. But it wouldn't be like that for long. Scarlett turned and walked as quickly and quietly as she could in the direction the beast had come, back towards the ravine. She'd have to figure out something soon, either to kill the thing or get out of these hills. Scarlett had not liked what she'd seen in the creature's eyes.

Hunger.

26

Brenna sat in the barracks, her armor on and locked into place. Around her, the other soldiers similarly suited up, but Brenna paid them no mind. Her gaze was fixed inward on an angry, simmering fire. She knew she should focus, knew she had to focus on the battle at hand. If they took down this Slaver camp, it would be a big success for the Eagles and they could start expanding their territory. It would be the first step towards removing the Slavers from the area altogether. But there was someone Brenna found herself hating more than the Slavers. No matter how she tried, she couldn't stop thinking about that girl. That stupid, fucking girl who had stolen her cream. Christ, did she have any idea how long it took Brenna to get that? What she had to do to acquire it? And then that girl went and used every last bit of it. There hadn't even been enough left to heal a poke from a single cactus needle. Thieving bitch.

A thought occurred to Brenna and she shifted slightly on the bench, still unseeing of the commotion around her. What if she could find a way to do her honor-bound duty to the Eagles and deliver some justice to that girl? Yeah, she went into the hills—and no one came out of the hills—but what if she was still alive? She had to have some skills if she'd managed to not only elude the grasp of the Slavers, but also escape during a firefight without so much as a knife. How had she gotten free in the first place? Probably Néron. That idiot and his personal honor code. He definitely would have helped her once the Slavers started shooting. He didn't like the idea of sitting ducks.

Brenna pulled out of her thoughts and glanced around the barracks. Most of the soldiers had begun to clear out, there were only a few stragglers still lacing their armor on the other side of the room. Brenna scanned the room, getting ready to stand and head out to the trucks, when her eyes landed on Néron. He was standing by the door. Watching her.

"What?" she asked, annoyed.

He shook his head.

"Nothing," Néron said.

"No, what is it?" she insisted. "Why are you watching me?"

"Because you look like you're thinking about making a mistake," Néron said.

"Excuse me?" Brenna asked, her eyes narrowing.

Néron didn't offer an explanation. Instead, he turned and left the barracks, followed shortly by the remaining soldiers. Alone, Brenna glared at where Néron had stood. They'd known each other for a long time, and Brenna sometimes found it unnerving that, at times, he seemed to know what she was thinking before she did. This time, however, he'd simply read her thoughts right off her face.

He didn't understand, Brenna decided. He had his rigid personal honor code which he never violated—and in turn, no one ever dishonored him like she had been dishonored. Not only had she been dishonored by that stupid thief, she had been humiliated. Brenna cringed and shifted uncomfortably on the bench as she recalled the High Elder's words.

"I suggest, Captain, that you drop this petty grievance and focus on the task at hand. Behave with the honor befitting your rank, else the council should be forced to . . . reconsider."

Angry tears threatened to release themselves once more, but Brenna swallowed hard, forcing her hurt back down. She decided there was only one way to correct this, only one way to balance the scales. During the battle, she would need to make her way into the hills. She'd go prepared with enough ammunition as a precaution for the beast, but she'd capture the girl and bring her back. Brenna would tie her hair to the back of the truck and drag her back to camp. Then there would be justice. Brenna could hand her over to the High Elder, and her personal honor would be restored.

Brenna rose to her feet. She readjusted her armor slightly and tightened the laces. She knew she'd have to be careful, but this was the only way. She knew it was the only way. Brenna walked towards the door, stopping by the gun rack to pick up the lone rifle that waited for her. She turned towards the empty barracks and held the gun to her shoulder, sighting the back corner of the room. She imagined that girl standing there, all smugness and arrogance.

"Pow, pow, pow," Brenna whispered, tapping the side of the trigger. "I've got you now, cunt."

Brenna smiled. She lowered the gun and slung it over her shoulder. She knew it would be difficult to steal away to the hills, so she'd have to wait for her moment. Brenna thought again of Néron and her smile faded. He might prove to be a more difficult challenge, but she'd face him later if she had to. If it came down to it, could she forcibly remove him from her path to redemption? Brenna didn't want it to come to that, but she thought she could if she had to. This was the only way.

27

Gray, pre-dawn light filtered down around Scarlett in the ravine as she surveyed the pile of bones once more. Ahead, she could see a cave. Jesus, thank god she'd gone left instead of right when she first climbed down into the ravine. Scarlett walked carefully around and occasionally over the bones as she looked for a weapon.

I'm sorry! I'm sorry! I'm sorry! she thought when there was no way for her to avoid stepping on some of the skeletal puzzle pieces. A rib cracked under her foot and Scarlett winced, both at the sound and at the human indignation of it all. *Maybe it was a Slaver's rib* she told herself. *You'd break one of those on purpose. This is fine. Suck it up.* Her guess about weapons had been correct in that there were a few strewn about the ravine, but most of them were as mangled as the broken bodies that had once housed the bones. Suddenly, a glint of silver caught Scarlett's eye. It was half-buried in the mud, but still, it gave Scarlett some hope. She quickly glanced up and down the ravine, searching for any sign of the creature, but there was none. The only movement she could see was the fog of her breath in the cold desert morning air. Scarlett knelt beside the piece of metal and dug her fingers into the cold mud, pulling it out by the handful. She shook it off, flinging it to the side, and dug in some more. She removed enough to wrap her hand around the smooth metal cylinder and pulled. It stuck for a moment before it gave way, popping out of the earth like a freshly freed tooth. Scarlett attempted to brush the mud off of the object but she mostly succeeded in just smearing it around. But she was able to clean it off enough to see what it was— a metal pole. Scarlett hadn't the faintest idea why someone had brought this in with them instead of something more effective like a sword or a bow and arrow, but it appeared to be the only item somewhat resembling a weapon that was currently intact. It'd do. Scarlett examined the ends and found one was somewhat sharp, although not terribly so. It'd be like stabbing the thing with a butter knife. However, if she could land a hit in the creature's eye, it could do some damage.

Scarlett looked over towards the cave. The opening was large and appeared tall enough for the beast to walk inside without having to duck down at all to avoid scraping its head. She let her eyes wander to the cliff above and saw several large there. They looked relatively secure from where she was standing, but nothing could be certain when it came to that sort of thing. Scarlett looked down at the pole in her hand and back up at the rocks. She then took the rope she'd saved and secured one end to her wrist, the other to the pole like a harpoon. Then she faced the ravine wall beside the cave. She wiped her muddy hands off on her legs and stomach as best she could, but some of the slick grit remained. Scarlett sighed and looked up at the wall, measuring the distance up towards the top of the cave. Despite the tiredness that wanted nothing more than to pull her down, she slowly found her footing on the wall and secured her fingertips on whatever purchase she could find. Bit by bit, inch by inch. The pole banged against her leg and pinged when it hit the rocks, but the rope held. When Scarlett reached the top of the cave, she braced herself against the solid rock and wedged the pole beneath the large, loose rocks she'd seen from down below. Her foot slipped a little and her stomach dropped before she caught herself. Breathing hard, she was thankful to realize the pole was still where she wanted it. Then, she was left with nothing to do but wait for the beast.

28

SCARLETT'S LEGS BEGAN to shiver from exhaustion. She had tried to stretch them out one at a time, but her individual legs weren't quite strong enough to hold her up alone, so she had abandoned that idea. The air was so cold and Scarlett wished yet again for a shirt or pants, anything to ward off the chill. Hell, she'd take a vest like that scout had worn. Or her boots. God, she wished she had shoes. She also wished she had some water. The cold air left her throat dry and scratchy, but the canteen across her back was still empty.

Then she saw it.

Scarlett saw the movement in the distance in the ravine, but she had to blink her eyes a few times to get them to focus properly. At first, she wasn't sure if she was really seeing it, but there it was: the beast. It looked larger and more fearsome in the early light, its dark eyes fixed on Scarlett. Suddenly, she wasn't cold anymore. Her legs still shook, but now it was from the adrenaline coursing through her veins. She took a deep breath and exhaled slowly, her breath whispering in the quiet air, the sound punctuated only by the approaching footsteps of the creature, crackling over the discarded bones. This was it. The animal drew closer and Scarlett saw its large teeth. *My, what big teeth you have* she thought. She couldn't remember where she knew that from, but she was sure it wasn't important. Leave it to her stupid brain to focus on something inconsequential at a time like this.

The beast drew closer, still watching Scarlett.

Come on, you son of a bitch she thought. *Closer. Come closer.*

The animal took another step forward. Then another. And another.

Scarlett sprang into action and dropped her full weight on the metal pole. She felt it bend and for a moment, she feared her plan might not work and she'd be left with a mangled, ineffective pole and a hungry beast. But then the rock wobbled. Scarlett pushed harder. Again it wobbled, but didn't give. The beast leaped up, its claws grating against the rock wall just below Scarlett's feet. Scarlett gave a primal yell and threw every last bit of strength she had into the pole. It bent further, but gave just enough. The rock fell. Scarlett reeled, windmilling her arms to keep from going over the edge, and fell back against the wall. The metal pole clattered over the edge. She heard a crack and a roar, loud and angry and long. Scarlett breathed hard. She'd done it. She'd actually done it. But . . . what had she done? Scarlett leaned forward and she although she couldn't be positive, it looked like the largest rock had landed on top of the animal. The beast roared again, but its voice sounded weaker, more pained. Scarlett edged back over to the ravine wall and slowly made her way down, her hands still shaking from adrenaline. She walked slowly, giving the animal a wide berth. It moaned again. The metal pole, nearly bent at a 90 degree angle, lay beside the creature. Scarlett steeled herself and took several deep breaths. *Do it. Do it. Do it. DO IT.*

Scarlett lunged forward and grabbed the pole before leaping backwards, tripping over her feet and landing hard on the ground. The beast looked over at her, its face full of pain. Scarlett climbed to her feet and inched closer, surveying the damage. The rock was in the middle of its back. Scarlett remembered the cracking sound she'd heard and winced. The animal looked up at her and put its head on the ground. Scarlett looked back to the pole in her hand and turned it so the sharp end was pointed at the thing's head. The beast watched her, unwilling to even pick up its head in protest. She aimed for its eye, ready to make a swift jab into the creature's head. Hopefully she could do it in one stab, she'd hate to have to do it in more. Scarlett steadied the pole, readjusting her grip. The animal looked from the pole to Scarlett's face, its eyes meeting hers. Scarlett locked her gaze on the animal's. *Do it. Do it. Just do it, god dammit. DO IT.*

Scarlett lowered the pole.

"Fuck!" she shouted, her voice echoing in the ravine. A handful of birds sprang out from one of the trees at the sound, fleeing into the dawn sky. The beast said nothing, but watched Scarlett with tired, defeated eyes.

"Fuck," Scarlett repeated, quieter this time. "Fuck, I just . . . I just can't."

The beast said nothing.

"Fuck you for keeping me treed all night though," Scarlett said to the animal, pointing a finger at its face. "That was a dick move."

She wasn't sure why part of her expected the animal to agree or say, "Oops, my bad." It did neither of those things and instead turned back to its own pain. Scarlett sighed and looked around. Well, what now? If she went back out the way she came, she was liable to walk back into that stupid fight between the Slavers and the feather people. God, she wanted something to drink. But what other way out did she have? She couldn't hide in here forever. Hell, she didn't even know if this was the only beast or not. She hadn't seen any others during the night, but that didn't mean they weren't elsewhere in the hills. Scarlett closed her eyes, thinking.

That's when she heard the water.

Scarlett opened her eyes and looked around. It sounded like running water. Faintly, but there it was. She took a cautious step towards the cave, straining her ears. Yes, there it was. She was sure of it. Scarlett looked back at the trapped beast.

"You bastard, you've been holding out on me," she said. The animal grumbled, but didn't apologize. Scarlett walked a few steps into the cave and paused. Inside, it wasn't completely dark. There were breaks in the roof of the cave and tiny shards of light littered across the cave floor. Scarlett held the pole at the ready, just in case. She took a few more steps inside, shuffling her bare feet carefully across the increasingly wet ground. Her right toes bumped up against something solid and . . . leather? Scarlett knelt down and felt around in the semi-darkness. She picked up the object and brought it over to one of the light fragments that shone through the cave ceiling.

"Oh my god," Scarlett said, examining what was in her hands. Either she was hallucinating or she was holding a quiver with a handful of arrows in it. The quiver had a deep gash in one side, but that didn't seem to affect its ability to hold its contents. She grabbed the arrows out in her anxious fist to examine them. Most of them were broken, their heads snapped off or the shafts splintered and useless. But three of the arrows were still in good shape. Scarlett hurried back to where she'd found it and dropped to her hands and knees, feeling around hopefully. Where there was a quiver, there might be a bow.

Scarlett crawled further and further away. Her fingertips brushed against something that shifted and she grabbed for it eagerly. Her hope fell when she discovered it was nothing more than a small and bumpy rock. It felt odd, and a little too symmetrical to be a regular rock. Scarlett squinted at it, bringing it closer to her eyes in the gloom. It was then that she realized she was holding a human vertebrae. Scarlett tossed it away and dry heaved, her throat involuntarily clenching and twisting. God, was a bow really worth it? Maybe she could just stab someone with the arrows and be done with it. She felt around cautiously, not wanting to touch any more skeletons than was absolutely necessary. She was just about to give up and keep moving when she felt something long and hard under her hand.

"Please don't be a bone, please don't be a bone, please don't be a bone," she whispered. She closed her hand around the object and picked it up, running her hands over its length. The bow. Scarlett mentally crossed her fingers and felt for a string, expecting it to be cut or just gone completely. Instead, it was there, as tight and secure as it should be. Scarlett sat back on her heels, holding the bow. Maybe her luck was changing. Scarlett didn't want to let herself get too optimistic, but hey, maybe this was the herald of a new era. Maybe she'd get really lucky and find some shoes.

Scarlett stood up and slung the quiver over her shoulder with the canteen. She headed back towards the centerline of the cave and continued moving deeper into its depths. The sound of running water grew louder and louder. Scarlett shuffled her feet a little faster, her mouth beginning to burn in desperation. She was close, so close to reaching the water. Then, suddenly, her toes were suspended in the air, the ground dropped out from beneath them. Scarlett cautiously lowered her foot and dipped it into the cool water that rushed over her toes. She knelt down, dropping the bow to the ground with a clatter, and scooped up some water in her cupped hands. She sipped it slowly, tasting the dirt that had clung to her fingers. As she drank, it occurred to Scarlett that if the water was running through the cave, it had to be coming from somewhere. Maybe, instead of going out the way she came into the hills and risking ending up in the middle of that stupid war, she could follow the water out to somewhere else, somewhere quieter. Maybe somewhere with shoes. Either way, it was worth a shot. But before she could do that, Scarlett wanted to sit by the water for just a little while. She pulled off the empty canteen and lowered it into the stream, letting the rushing water fill the container before she set it down beside her. Then Scarlett lay down beside the stream, trailing her fingers in the water. Perhaps she could close her eyes, just for a minute. Scarlett knew that was stupid, there could be more animals around, but her body was beginning to shut down. Her eyes were heavy and she sank down further and further into her body until she drifted away into a dreamless, fitful sleep.

29

GRUN PULLED THE whip back towards him, snaking across the ground like a rattler. He ran his hand over it, wiping off the scout's blood as he did so. It ran over his knuckles like red tears before they dripped to the ground between his feet. He waited a moment, watching the piteous woman tied spread eagled between two posts in the center of the arena as she sobbed. *Spread eagled.* Grun smirked at the thought. Christ, he wanted to eviscerate every last one of them. Soon enough, he reminded himself as he looked over the scout. Soon enough. The lash marks were like angry ribbons wrapped around the scout's buttocks and legs. Grun smiled. He liked it when they cried.

"Now I'm going to ask you again," Grun said as he circled around her. Should he start lashing her front? He waffled a bit as he examined her. Maybe not quite yet. Grun continued his circle until he was standing behind her once more. "What is the Eagles' attack strategy?"

"I," the scout tried to say, her voice shaking with pain. "I—I don't know. I didn't hear anything."

Grun's whip hit her back with a crack and the scout screamed, her voice breaking in the middle as the pain overtook her. The crowd of Slavers in the stands cheered approvingly. Tension lined the ropes tied to her wrists as the scout's knees buckled involuntarily, but she couldn't go far.

"I told you, I don't like that answer," Grun said, drawing lazy circles in the dirt with the whip.

"I—I'm sorry," the scout sobbed, forcing the words out of her throat. Speaking seemed to cause her immense pain, which Grun rather enjoyed. He walked around her, eyeing her wounds. She probably couldn't handle much more at the moment, not if he wanted to keep her alive. But she could probably take a little more.

"I'm not interested in your apologies," Grun said as he walked back around to look her in the eyes. She tried to raise them, pain attempting to force them closed. When her eyes finally met his, Grun raised his arm and delivered a powerful backhanded slap to her right cheek. The onlookers cheered as her lip split. Grun cocked his head for a moment, listening to the crowd.

"Fuck her up!"

"Gouge out her eyes!"

"Kill her!"

"Stick a knife in her belly!"

"Stick a knife up her cunt!"

Grun smiled at the suggestions, but raised his hand for silence. The noise in the crowd dropped immediately to whispers and then nothing at all.

"This disgusting creature," Grun said loudly, turning to face the audience, "is a traitor. She disobeyed direct orders from her master and defected to the Eagles. And now," Grun said, circling the scout like a cat circling its prey, "she has been recaptured."

The crowd cheered. Only a handful knew that the stupid bitch had actually run back to them in the middle of a firefight, but Grun wasn't worried. The people would believe what they were told to believe, and a handful of contradictors would be easy enough to deal with. If they dared contradict him at all. What was important was to encourage this narrative; she had disobeyed and she had betrayed, so now she must pay.

"I'm not going to kill her," Grun announced. The crowd groaned in disappointment. "Yet. She might still have valuable information locked in that stupid, fucking skull of hers," Grun said, tapping her head with the butt of his whip to emphasize each word. "My whip doesn't seem to have loosened her tongue," Grun continued, chucking her under the chin with the whip before he started to loop it in his hands, "but I have an idea to help, shall we say, get the conversation flowing."

Grun tossed the whip to a nearby Slaver who immediately dropped it into the dirt. Grun briefly closed his eyes. Christ, these fuckers were such idiots. Grun opened them again and motioned towards the shadows near the arena's entrance. The Pet stepped out into the light, her rifle slung across her back. Grun could see a knife attached to a cord around her waist. Perfect. At the sight of The Pet, the crowd began to mumble uncomfortably. A few people laughed nervously. Grun surveyed the crowd and saw a few men watching hungrily, waiting to see what The Pet would do. Grun grinned. He loved that she inspired so much fear and that everyone knew she symbolized raw violence. A worrying thought occurred to him and his smile faltered a little. God, what would happen if The Pet was incapacitated in the fight today? He knew she could more than handle herself, but she wasn't invincible against an army. Maybe he should do what he could to protect her, keep her off to the side, use her as a sharpshooter. Without her, he knew his position as Grand Master could be compromised. He couldn't let that happen.

Grun shook off his thoughts as The Pet approached. Later. He'd have to think about that later. But for now, the compound was watching. The Pet came to a stop in front of him, standing at attention, awaiting further instructions. Grun reached out and turned her by the shoulders until The Pet was facing the bleeding, now semi-conscious scout.

"Do you see her?" Grun asked softly, murmuring to The Pet through her helmet.

She nodded her head.

"Do you see her skin?" he asked.

She nodded again. Grun could hear her breath beneath the helmet, heavier now.

"Do you like it?" Grun asked, sliding a hand around her waist.

The Pet nodded again, her breathing lustful and thick.

"Would you like to play with it?" he whispered as he pulled her knife from its sheath.

The Pet's breathing began to speed up, sounding nearly orgasmic. Grun ran the flat side of the blade across The Pet's stomach before he placed the knife gently in her hand. Her fingers closed tightly around it.

"Not too deep," he instructed softly. "We're saving her for later."

The Pet nodded, her muscles tense and ready to pounce.

"Good girl," Grun whispered. He released The Pet and the crowd cheered. And then the scout began to scream in earnest.

30

Néron climbed into one of the waiting trucks, glancing over his shoulder towards the barracks. Brenna still hadn't come out. He wasn't sure what she was planning, but whatever it was, he knew it was likely a bad idea. He suspected she was still stewing over that girl, Scarlett, and Néron was afraid Brenna was going to do something insane, like go into the Blood Hills. Normally, Néron knew that wasn't something Brenna would ever do. But lately, something was . . . off. Brenna frequently looked like she hadn't slept, the circles under her eyes growing darker and darker. And not just in the last couple days. This had started weeks ago, and it was getting harder for Néron to recognize her. Rash, impulsive, angry—it was so unlike her. Usually, she was so calm and level-headed. It was what made her a great captain. But now, she was deteriorating in front of his eyes. Then there were those rumors of the Elders' stores being robbed at night, the locks broken. Néron hadn't wanted to believe Brenna was capable of something like that, but then where had she gotten that cream? She'd said she traded for it, but now Néron wasn't so sure. This obsession with Scarlett wasn't like her either. Perhaps he'd better keep an eye on Brenna during the battle. Just in case.

Brenna finally emerged from the barracks and jogged towards the waiting trucks, a rifle slung over her shoulder. Néron tried to catch her eye, but she pointedly ignored him, taking her seat up front. He watched the back of her head and noticed the tension in her neck. Resolute. He'd seen her this way before battles in the past, but something was different this time and he didn't like it at all.

"Eagles!" the general yelled as she climbed atop one of the trucks at the front of the company. "The time has come once more for us to take on those that seek to destroy us. The Slavers have been a constant thorn in our heel, and now is the time to put a stop to this. Today is surely only the first step in what will be a lengthy war, but if we can take this Slaver compound, that is one more foothold in our land as we take back what is rightfully ours."

The Eagles cheered in agreement, theirs yells loud and raucous.

"It is important to remember," the general continued as the cheering faded, "that the Slavers are a violent tribe built on hate and destruction. They serve only themselves and they will do whatever deceitful, disgraceful thing necessary to accomplish that goal. But we are not Slavers," the general said. The company nodded approvingly. "We are Eagles. We have fortitude. We have integrity. We have, above all, honor."

"Yes!" cried out several Eagles in agreement. "Yes!"

"As is custom before going into battle," the general said, "I want to remind you of that honor that we serve, that honor that we fight for with every breath in our bodies."

"We honor and serve the mission laid out before us. We will fight, without ceasing, to bring victory," the general called out. "We honor and protect our sisters and brothers in arms, never abandoning them. We rise as one flock, one bird, one feather. United, we are unstoppable, and we honor the Eagles with every breath we take."

The general closed her right hand into a fist and thumped it in the middle of her chest. The company did the same, echoing her vow. She roared over the silent company, a loud, long, primal yell that rose up from her feet. The company responded, roaring back like dozens of angry lions.

"Let's go!" the general yelled. The company cheered as the general climbed down from the roof of the truck and took her place inside the cab. The engines of the trucks revved to life, adding power to the roars of the Eagles. Néron felt his blood run faster though his veins, the adrenaline coursing through his body. He closed his hand around the red feather that hung on a cord around his neck and he shut his eyes. *We rise as one flock, one bird, one feather. United, we are unstoppable, and I honor the Eagles with every breath I take.*

Néron opened his eyes again and centered his thoughts in the present, feeling every bump from every rock as the trucks crossed the desert. His shoulders jostled between his comrades on either side of him and it made him think of a river, all of the water flowing as one. Néron looked through the rear window of the truck cab at the back of Brenna's head. One cup of water still felt discordant. Néron hoped she wouldn't do anything foolish. If she did, he couldn't be held accountable for what he would have to do to bring her back to the Elders. But Brenna knew the score: above all else, Eagles and honor. However, knowing the score doesn't always mean one continues to play the game correctly. Néron did not want to have to be the one to correct Brenna, but he would do it without hesitation if it came to that.

Above all else, Eagles and honor.

31

THE SCOUT'S BODY felt like it was on fire. Her arms were practically in ribbons and she wondered how she wasn't dead yet. Everything hurt, everything. God, why hadn't they just let her die?

"Coming, Hawk?" Roan asked.

"No," Hawk said, exasperated. "I have to stay here and guard this stupid cunt."

"What?" Roan asked, confused. "Why?"

Hawk shrugged.

"Beats me."

The scout's vision began to close, the edges fuzzing into darkness. Was she dying? Oh, Christ, she hoped so.

"Say, Hawk . . ." Roan started. He glanced around and took a step closer to Hawk, confidentially lowering his voice. "What do you think of the Grand Master?"

"What about him?" Hawk asked, lowering his voice to match Roan's volume.

"I mean . . . well, what do you think about him as a leader?" Roan asked.

"Why do you ask?" Hawk asked cautiously, glancing at the scout.

As she blacked out, the scout became vaguely aware that her body didn't hurt anymore. *Please, please let this be it.*

"Oh, don't worry about her, she's either unconscious or dead," Roan said, gesturing to the scout.

"I don't think he'd order me to guard her if she was dead," Hawk said doubtfully.

"What does he want with her anyway?" Roan asked. "Why not just let The Pet finish her off?"

Hawk shrugged.

"Beats me."

"But, really," Roan asked, lowering his voice again. "What do you think of Grun?"

Hawk considered this question.

"I'm not sure," Hawk said thoughtfully. "Why do you ask?"

"Well," Roan said, dropping his voice to a loud whisper. "There's been . . . talk."

"What sort of talk?" Hawk whispered back.

Roan stared at him for a long minute.

"Can I trust you?" Roan asked.

"Sure you can," Hawk said. "Brotherhood."

"Brotherhood," Roan echoed. He paused, licking his dry lips. "There's been talk that Grun might not be right for his position," Roan said.

"How so?" Hawk asked.

"What has he really done to strengthen the Slavers?" Roan asked. "I mean really strengthen us?"

"We're about to go to war with the Eagles," Hawk replied. "That's something."

"Yes, but have we made any progress against them until now?" Roan asked.

"What do you mean?" Hawk asked.

"Our last major battle was a decade ago," Roan said.

"I thought we were building up our military reserves," Hawk said.

"Have you seen any real, notable growth in our forces?" Roan asked.

Hawk thought about this for a moment.

"Now that you mention it . . . no," Hawk admitted.

"Then what have we been doing all this time?" Roan asked. "It seems our fearless leader has just been enjoying the spoils of being at the top without actually doing anything to benefit the Slavers."

"Where are you going with this?" Hawk asked.

"There's been . . . talk," Roan said.

"You said that."

"Talk of . . . shall we say, replacing Grun."

"With who?"

Roan sighed.

"That part is up for debate. A lot of us want the position."

"I wouldn't mind taking a shot at it," Hawk said brightly.

Roan barely resisted the urge to roll his eyes.

"Well, whoever is going to do it, there's no way we could get past The Pet," Roan said. "Unless . . ."

"Unless what?"

"Unless something were to happen to her during this battle with the Eagles."

"Like what?"

Roan smacked Hawk on the back of the head.

"Ow!" Hawk exclaimed, rubbing the back of his head. "That hurt."

"Oh, suck it up," Roan said. "And what do you think I mean about something happening to The Pet?"

"You mean like we kill her?" Hawk asked, looking uncomfortable. "I don't know, she's . . . she's scary."

Roan shuddered.

"God, she gives me the fucking creeps," Roan said, glancing around to be sure no one else had entered the arena. "No, not us. Not yet, anyway. But maybe we could . . . I don't know, ensure she doesn't come back from the fight. Get the Eagles to take her down."

"Do you think they could?" Hawk asked doubtfully.

"She can't hold up against an entire army," Roan said.

"What makes you think they'd go after her in the first place?" Hawk asked.

"Because if you want to kill a beast, you have to rip out its heart," Roan said.

"I don't think it's necessary to rip out the heart in order to kill something," Hawk said thoughtfully.

"You're missing the point," Roan growled, exasperated.

"What's your point then?" Hawk asked.

"My point is that we need to make sure The Pet is vulnerable to the Eagles during this fight."

"What if they don't kill her?" Hawk asked.

"Then we'll have to be ready with a backup plan," Roan said, although his confidence seemed to falter a little at the idea of having to deal with The Pet himself.

Hawk shuddered.

"Are you in?" Roan asked, glancing around again to be sure no one was listening.

"Yeah," said Hawk. "I'm in."

Roan grinned and clapped Hawk on the back before he turned and left the arena. A drop of blood fell from the tip of the scout's middle finger, forming a perfect sphere before it splashed across the dirt below. Someone else, lurking unseen in the shadows, retied the laces on her boots before she straightened her helmet and snuck out of the arena behind Roan. Hawk saw nothing and scuffed his boots in the dirt by the scout, once more bored by his posting.

32

"SON OF A BITCH!" Scarlett growled through gritted teeth as she lowered herself into the cold water. After following the water's path through the increasingly narrow cave, Scarlett was forced to continue along in the water. Christ, she hoped this would turn into something useful to get her out of the hills and away from those psychos in the desert. She just wished the water weren't so goddamn cold. The water was deeper than she'd anticipated, nearly reaching her armpits. Scarlett had to concentrate to keep her footing on the slick stones at the bottom, her balance uncertain in the deeper water. The quiver of bows was slung across her back and Scarlett remembered, too late, the rip in the quiver.

"Well, fuck," she said aloud. Scarlett paused in the water and pulled the quiver off of her body, dumping water on her head in the process. She sighed and felt like punching someone. She examined the quiver and debated for a moment about what to do. If she kept it on her back in the water, she risked losing the arrows and with only three, she couldn't afford that. But if she carried it along with the bow, that was going to be a pain in the ass to try and keep them out of the water. Scarlett sighed again. Carrying it was. Keeping the arrows was more important.

Scarlett made her way down the waterway and the water gradually got deeper and deeper until it was up to her neck. She hesitated, wondering if she should turn back. Fuck it, too late now.

"God dammit, Mel," Scarlett said aloud as she tiptoed forward in the water. "God *fucking* dammit. I can't believe you dropped me in the *fucking* desert. No hard feelings, my ass. Now I'm in the *fucking* water and I might drown in here or get eaten by a mutant beast or get shot by Slavers or fucking feather people. I don't know what the *fuck* your problem is, but—"

Scarlett's words were cut off as the ground beneath her careful steps disappeared and her head dropped below the surface. She popped up again, sputtering water. Well, so much for keeping the bow and arrows dry. Scarlett swam back against the current until her toes could touch the bottom of the waterway and hooked the bow across her back with the canteen, which she regretted filling so soon as it just acted as a weight in the water. She kept the quiver in her hand and took a breath before she paddled forward. The current helped to carry her forward and for a moment, Scarlett found herself enjoying the swim. She'd always liked swimming. As she continued on through the cave's river, Scarlett found herself thinking of another day, another swim. She and Mel had just finished a job and they'd felt good. Very good. They'd stopped by a riverbank to eat in the later afternoon sun. Scarlett had felt warm and happy in the mead-colored light as the sun smoldered into a sunset.

"Come on," Mel had said, brushing the crumbs from her hands as she stood.

"Come on where?" Scarlett had asked. "We don't need to be anywhere."

Mel didn't say anything but grinned instead. She walked closer to the water's edge, stripping off her gear and then her clothes, dropping everything into a pile. When she was naked, she'd waded into the river, leaning her head back to dip her hair. Scarlett had smiled as she watched her.

"Coming?" Mel had asked innocently.

Scarlett had stood up and followed Mel's lead, dropping everything before joining her in the water. The water had been warm from the sun, and as the pinks and oranges in the sky faded to blues and purples, Scarlett and Mel had been happy.

Scarlett shoved the memory from her mind, annoyed. She was not in the mood to deal with a happy trip down memory lane. She was already pissed off for being in this stupid fucking situation and she knew she had to keep her emotions in check. Out of control emotions led you to make stupid decisions. They kept you from thinking clearly. If she let her mind go to Mel, really go to Mel, Scarlett was afraid she'd do something stupid and then the past few days of fighting for her life would be for naught.

Scarlett swam further, focusing as hard as she could on the present moment, on the feel of the water on her skin, on the sound of her splashes as she pushed forward. Then she saw something directly ahead of her that made her pause: a wall. The current carried her to it and Scarlett bumped against the stone. Below, she could feel the current pushing forward down by her ankles. Still keeping a hand on the wall, Scarlett experimentally pushed her feet forward feeling for an opening. Her toes traced an opening that was narrow, but not impossible for her to fit through, even with the bow. But how long would she have to be in the tunnel? What was on the other side? Scarlett hesitated, glancing back the way she'd come. There wouldn't be any light down there. There wasn't a lot of light in here either, but the little breaks in the roof of the cave had given her something. Down there . . . there was nothing. Scarlett steeled herself for a moment, considering her options.

"Fuck!" she shouted, her voice echoing in the cave. She felt a little better. Scarlett then took a big gulp of air and ducked down below the water's cold surface. She kept her eyes open but it was dark in the tunnel. Scarlett moved easily, using her hands to guide her through. The current helped to propel her forward as her lungs began to burn.

Then she stopped.

Don't panic, don't panic, don't panic Scarlett repeated to herself. *Focus*. Scarlett felt around and realized the end of the bow was stuck on a rock. The current was stronger now, making it harder to pull the bow against it to free herself. The tunnel was narrow enough to where Scarlett wasn't sure she could wiggle out of the bow and leave it behind. *Fuck fuck fuck fuck FUCK* Scarlett screamed in her head, her lungs aching now. She released a tiny stream of bubbles which helped a little, but only served to remind her of how badly she wanted new air. Scarlett could feel lightheadedness seeping in and she forced herself to focus. She could not pass out here. After all she'd been through, she refused to fucking drown. Finally, in a burst of adrenaline, Scarlett shoved against the current and yanked the bow free. The water's momentum pushed her forward and Scarlett felt relieved for a moment before she stopped again. Scarlett groped frantically behind her and felt the canteen wedged against a rock. She braced herself against the tunnel walls and then launched off with her arms and legs as hard as she could. The canteen strap ripped and Scarlett felt it tumble and hit her ankle before disappearing into the darkness. Scarlett started moving forward again, but this was no time to celebrate. She was still in the tunnel. She might be free, but there was still no air. *Stay focused* Scarlett told herself, using everything she had to concentrate on kicking her feet, one after the other as she groped blindly in the dark underwater tunnel. She wasn't going to make it. Fuck, she wasn't going to make it. She never should have gone down into the tunnel, she should've just taken her odds against the fucking feather people. She should have—

The tunnel suddenly widened and she could see light filtering into the water ahead. Light! Light meant surface. Light meant air. Oh, fuck, if this was an artificial light under the water she was going to be so pissed. Scarlett kicked hard, propelling herself forward and up as her already limited vision began to darken at the edges.

Then, she broke the surface.

Scarlett immediately sucked in a huge breath of air and started coughing, a horrible hacking sound that nearly turned into retching as she gasped for air. She turned onto her back, somehow still holding the quiver with three arrows against her stomach, and floated for a little way, the current slower now, getting her breath back. She'd done it. She'd made it. As her breathing calmed, she began to take in her surroundings. She was in some kind of underground waterway, although there were lights installed along the walls above her. Scarlett was about to turn over to stop floating and begin swimming again when he head suddenly smacked into something hard.

"Ow, shit!" she exclaimed, flipping over in the water. She looked over to see what she'd hit, expecting only to see the wall, but was instead greeted by a metal ladder. She grabbed hold of one of the rungs and looked up. There, above her, was some kind of grate. Her muscles protested, but Scarlett hoisted herself out of the water, climbing carefully up the ladder. Her wet feet threatened to slip off at any given moment, but Scarlett went slowly, the quiver's strap slung over one arm. When she reached the grate, she paused, squinting through the narrow slats. She couldn't see much of anything other than a single light hanging over the grate.

It's either this or back into the water she told herself.

Scarlett hooked her legs around the ladder as tightly as she could in order to free her hands, the metal rungs pressing painfully against the backs of her knees. She put both hands on the grate, praying it wasn't bolted down, and pushed. At first, it didn't move, but then she gave another shove and it wavered under her hands. Scarlett pushed again, hard, and she managed to raise the grate enough to put one end up on the floor above. She gripped the ladder with one hand, relaxing her legs for a moment. Then she used her free hand to push again, making the opening a little bigger. Finally, she pushed the grate aside enough to allow her to wiggle up through the ceiling, her side scraping against the grate's hard edge. Scarlett sat on the floor for a moment, panting hard, before she pulled the grate back into place, the slats sharp against her fingers.

The room wasn't much. There were several tables and chairs stacked haphazardly around her, so Scarlett assumed it was storage. But whose storage was it? Scarlett stood up and pulled the bow off of her back, and she noticed the bow's string left an angry red line cutting diagonally across her torso. Of course. Scarlett slung the quiver across her back once more, splashing out the remaining water across the floor, and pulled out an arrow. She crept across the room and put her ear to the door, listening for something, anything. Nothing. Scarlett reached for the door handle and turned it slowly, praying the door didn't have an alarm. She couldn't imagine anyone wanted to protect a handful of tables and chairs with an alarm, but you never knew. Some people were fucking weird.

The handle turned smoothly and Scarlett cracked open the door, relieved to remain in silence. There was a hallway on the other side of the door, and a seemingly empty one at that. Scarlett was about to open the door further and let herself out when she suddenly heard the sound of boots on the hard floor. She froze, flattening herself against the wall, but she left the door open. Shutting it now might draw undue attention to it, and the last thing she needed right now was some kind of confrontation with somebody who hadn't been expecting her. Scarlett waited, her breath slow and measured and silent.

The footsteps passed Scarlett without pause and began to fade down the hallway. Scarlett took a risk and cautiously poked her head out to look after the person who possessed the boots. Her heart sank when she saw the black pants and vest and shaved head of the retreating man. Scarlett wanted to scream in frustration, but kept silent. She closed the door as silently as she could and sat back against the wall in her storage room, exhaling a measured breath to help maintain her temper. Okay, so ending up in a Slaver building wasn't great. Actually, it was super shitty, but at least she wasn't drowning. And now she also had a weapon. Scarlett looked down at the bow in her hands, running her hands along its wooden handle. Only three arrows, but that was three more than she'd had earlier. Technically, she had a 300% increase in sharp projectiles, so that was something.

Right?

Scarlett glanced back towards the grate in the floor. Maybe the water hadn't been that bad. I mean, really, how close had she *actually* been to drowning? Scarlett sighed. At least up here, she was on land. What she wouldn't give for a set of gills . . .

Scarlett stood up resolutely. Enough fucking around. She was going to find some goddamn clothes and get the fuck out of here. Scarlett quietly turned the door handle once more and peeked into the hallway. Empty. She prepped an arrow in the bow and stepped into the hall.

33

Scarlett's feet were nearly silent on the cold hallway tile, anticipation thundering in her ears with her heartbeat. With only three arrows, she knew she had to be conservative, but she still felt like she might have a hard time resisting the urge to fire an arrow into the eye of the first Slaver she saw. Maybe she'd get lucky and she'd be able to justify it. *Well,* of course *I had to shoot him in the eye and stomp on his dick, it was self defense! He would've eventually woken up from his nap and seen me, and then WHO KNOWS what would've happened?!* Scarlett smirked in spite of herself. She didn't enjoy killing just for the sake of killing, but apparently spending a few days naked in the desert could uncover all sorts of things about one's personality.

Scarlett came to the end of the hallway and pressed her back against the wall, pausing for a moment before she peeked her head around the corner. Down to her left was a single Slaver with a rifle slung across his back, leaning against a wall and looking bored. Scarlett ducked back into her hallway and took a deep breath. She had the element of surprise, but a bow was no match for a gun. She'd have one shot and she had to make it count. Scarlett took in one more deep breath for good luck. *Good air in, 2, 3, 4, bad air out, 2, 3, 4.*

Scarlett whipped around the corner and the arrow was rocketing towards the Slaver before he even knew what was happening. The arrow cleanly pierced the Slaver's neck and he went down, clutching at his throat. He looked around desperately for his attacker and saw a naked woman with long dark hair quickly advancing towards him. He lunged towards her but fell hard on his knees, swiping ineffectively at her legs.

Scarlett watched him for a moment, waiting for him to go down. She quickly grew bored waiting for him to die and pulled another arrow from the damp, torn quiver. The Slaver stared at her, trying to choke out a yell, but all that came out was a wet gurgle. Scarlett shot him through the eye and, after a gruesome moment, the Slaver fell forward, the arrow in his eye snapping in two when it hit the tile. Scarlett grimaced, but tossed down her bow and immediately set to work pulling the rifle from the dead man. Scarlett grunted under the man's weight as she lifted him up slightly to tug the rifle strap free. The strap momentarily stuck on the arrow protruding from the Slaver's neck, but she managed to unhook it and she dropped the Slaver to the tile floor with a thud. Scarlett raised the rifle to her shoulder and sighted it, looking up and down the empty hallway.

Finally.

The gun felt good in her hands, familiar, like she'd just reattached a limb. Scarlett checked the magazine—only half full. She shrugged. It wasn't great, but it was better than what she'd had for the last few days. Scarlett looked down at the dead man by her feet, the puddle of blood seeping from his head and neck getting dangerously close to her toes. She took a step back and sighted the rifle at the man's head. Part of her wanted to pull the trigger, wanted to feel the kick of the rifle so badly after so many days without one. But that seemed like overkill at this point and honestly, hadn't she left a big enough trail in her wake over the past few days? The last thing she needed to do was fire off a rifle in a hallway and alert a whole building of Slavers to her presence. Actually, the smart thing to do at that moment would be to not only refrain from shooting a dead guy in the head, but to get the fuck out of a hallway where she was extremely exposed. She might have a gun, but she was still naked.

Scarlett walked quickly down the hall. At the end she checked around the corner, but saw no one. This struck her as a little odd that the halls were so devoid of people, but for the moment, she decided to just go with it. She knew that if Slavers weren't here, they were all probably somewhere else and with her luck, she was going to walk right into their slumber party.

After carefully stalking her way through several more hallways, Scarlett finally found a door that led outside. She peeked through the glass in the door and surveyed the situation. Again, the area was largely devoid of people. She cracked open the door and listened. A warm wind blew through the compound and in the distance, Scarlett could hear shouting. As long as she kept her ears open, she should be able to listen for any impending Slavers. God, she just wanted to find some clothes and get the fuck out of there. She briefly considered staying in the building and searching for something to wear, but she knew she'd probably pushed her luck too far already. Instead, Scarlett took a deep breath and snuck out into the warm sunshine. The air felt good on her skin, a pleasant contrast to the chilly building and cold water from down below.

Before her, the path from the building diverged into three choices: left, right, or straight. Scarlett listened carefully, surveying the area. Still no one in sight, but she knew that wouldn't last for long. She thought the shouting was coming from up ahead, so that was out, which left one turn or the other. Scarlett was about to flip a mental coin when she heard the sound of footsteps coming from the left. *Well, that was easy.* Scarlett took off toward the right, staying as low as she could. As she rounded the building, she saw what looked like some kind of outdoor arena up ahead. God only knew what those Slavers considered sport. But the entryway was shaded and she'd be able to regroup and figure out a plan of action if she stopped there. Scarlett dashed across the dirt paths, wincing each time her foot hit a small rock. *There better be some fucking shoes in that arena.*

Safely in shadow, Scarlett glanced back out at the pathways. The footsteps she'd heard didn't appear to have followed her to this side of the building and she felt relieved. God, how was anyone supposed to get out of this stupid compound? She was about to head back out into the light when she glanced into the arena. She saw a bored looking guard, sitting on the ground and leaning up beside a post. Then she realized what was strung up between the guard's backrest and a second post: a woman, beaten and bloodied. The woman's arms were dark red, clotted with blood. She wore an outfit just like that scout from before had worn, and, judging by the way Scarlett had seen her earlier, this woman's backside was probably beat to hell. Scarlett squinted at the woman between the two posts, trying to make out her face. When she realized it was one she recognized, Scarlett stared in disbelief.

"Oh, what the fuck?" Scarlett groaned, trying to keep her voice down so as not to alert the guard. Really? Again? Fuck, this chick must be a glutton for punishment. *And apparently, so am I* Scarlett thought. She put the gun up to her shoulder and headed into the arena.

34

WHILE STUDYING HIS cuticles, the guard never saw Scarlett coming until just before she smashed the butt of her gun in his face.

"What the fuck?!" Hawk shouted as his nose crunched and blood spurted across his face.

Scarlett responded by cracking him on the skull again with the gun, knocking Hawk into the dirt. Hawk clutched at his head, doubled over in pain. Scarlett took the opportunity to snag the knife from his belt and cut the strap of his gun, disarming him. While Hawk moaned on the ground, Scarlett checked the magazine on his rifle. Full. Excellent. Scarlett took the clip and swapped it with hers before slinging her gun on her back and putting Hawk's to her shoulder with the half-full clip and pointing it at him.

"I'll kill you for that!" Hawk exclaimed through bleary eyes, his vision dotted with blood.

"The fuck you will," Scarlett said. "Now what the fuck happened here?" she asked, gesturing to the scout.

"Grand Master said to guard her," Hawk said, spitting a tooth into the dirt.

Scarlett picked up her foot and kicked him in the neck with her heel. Hawk shouted in pain.

"I don't give a fuck what you're doing! I can see what you're doing, you fucking idiot!" she exclaimed. "I meant what happened to her?" she asked, gesturing to the scout again.

"Grand Master and The Pet," Hawk said as he sat down again, leaning his head against the post once more.

Scarlett glared at him.

"I don't live in your fucked up little world, none of that makes any sense to me."

"The Grand Master is our leader. Well, for now anyway," Hawk said. "There's probably going to be a coup later."

Scarlett ignored the last part.

"What's The Pet?" she asked.

In spite of his new injuries, Hawk shuddered.

"I . . . I don't want to talk about it," he said, gingerly touching his neck and nose.

"Well, whatever happened, it's over. I'm taking her," Scarlett said. She pulled the magazine from Hawk's rifle and tossed it away, far out of his reach. Then she took the knife and began to cut the ropes that bound the scout.

"Hey, you can't do that!" Hawk protested.

Scarlett didn't say anything, but instead swung her rifle around from her back and shot him in the kneecap. Hawk screamed.

"Would you keep it down?" she asked calmly as she resumed cutting down the scout. "All your yelling is rather distracting."

"You fucking shot me!" Hawk shouted at her.

"Well, you had it coming," Scarlett said as she hoisted the scout over her shoulder.

"Fucking bitch!" Hawk managed to wheeze before he started dry heaving at the sight of what his knee had become. Scarlett turned to leave the arena, but remembered one more piece of information she needed.

"Hey, where do you keep the clothes?" Scarlett asked, shifting the scout's weight on her shoulder. God, they'd really done a number on her, her legs were a mess. Even worse than the first time she'd found her. Scarlett tried not to focus on the wounds and looked back at Hawk. Shit, she probably should've just taken his pants, but now they were covered in pieces of kneecap and cartilage. Gross.

"What?" Hawk asked, barely able to focus on Scarlett's words. She narrowed her eyes, feeling entirely too sick of this shit to put up with it anymore.

"WHERE THE FUCK ARE THE CLOTHES?" Scarlett screamed at him, pointing the rifle at his remaining kneecap. Hawk froze, his eyes wide. In the distance, there was a smattering of gunfire, but neither Hawk nor Scarlett looked away from one another.

"Main building," Hawk said, pointing towards the direction from which she'd come. "Second floor, third door on your left at the top of the stairs."

"Thank you," Scarlett said, her tone as icy as her stare. With that, she turned and left the arena with the scout, ignoring Hawk's whimpering cries behind her.

35

THE EAGLE TRUCKS roared as they approached the Slaver compound, sprinting forward like desert cats towards their prey. From her seat in the truck's cab, Brenna stared at the Slaver's walled citadel. She tried to focus on the battle at hand, but found her gaze wandering off towards the Blood Hills. That woman was dead in there, she had to be. No one survived the Blood Hills. Brenna had never been inside herself, but she'd heard the beast's roar echoing across the desert at night. But that stupid bitch was resourceful—what if she wasn't dead? Brenna hated not knowing. She jiggled her leg anxiously as the trucks drew nearer to the compound.

"Nervous?" the driver asked, glancing over at Brenna's fidgety leg.

"No," Brenna said, shaking her head as she willed her leg to stop moving. "Angry."

"At least you'll get to take it out on some Slavers in a moment," the driver said.

"Yes," Brenna agreed, glancing over towards the hills once more.

Suddenly, a bullet shattered the windshield and lodged itself in the driver's neck. The driver spluttered, searching for words, but found none as the truck swerved violently, nearly sideswiping another Eagle truck. Brenna grabbed the wheel and tried to straighten the vehicle as she kicked over and jammed her foot on the brake pedal, yanking hard on the emergency brake with her free hand. The truck screeched horribly and the smell of burning rubber filled Brenna's nose, but it stopped. Another shot cracked the windshield and Brenna ducked, bits of glass raining down into her hair. She dove out of the truck and ran around to the back where Néron and the other Eagles were already disembarking, some returning fire towards the compound. The other trucks stopped around them, creating a sort of refuge from the bullets.

"Remember the strategy!" the general yelled, her voice barely audible over the gunfire. "Get inside, take the compound, and destroy anyone who gets in your way."

Slavers began to spill out of the front of the compound, like wine out of an overturned bottle. Brenna swung her rifle around to the front and pressed the butt of it to her shoulder, sighting it towards the top of the compound wall. She picked off three Slavers in quick succession before she pulled her eye away from the scope. She watched a wall of Slavers clash with Eagles, knives out, guns out, war cries mixed with gun fire as blood ran across the dry desert earth. Brenna scanned the war zone and realized after a moment that she was searching for that thief. *Bitch*. Logically,

Brenna knew there was no way that woman would be in a fight helping the Slavers. There's no way in hell they'd have ever given her a gun and if she was here, she was probably locked up somewhere.

Hey, that was something. What if she was here? Maybe she'd come out of the hills and the Slavers had gotten ahold of her. Brenna could find her and deal with her that way. God, how easy would that be? All the hard work would already be done. She raised her rifle and picked off a Slaver running full tilt towards the trucks. He pitched forward, flailing as he did so in an almost comical way, before what was left of his face hit the dirt. Brenna glanced over towards the hills. As much as she'd like for that woman to be here, no one came out of the hills. God, all she needed was 20 minutes in there, 30 at the most. Brenna scanned the fight and tried to gauge the distance from the fight to the hills. There was no way she could take a truck, she knew that. But what if she could get ahold of a Slaver bike? She could zip over there, grab the thief or at least confirm she was dead, then come back and finish this. Yes, that could work. It'd have to.

Brenna glanced over and noticed Néron watching her out of the corner of his eye.

"What?" Brenna demanded, irritated. "Don't you have something better to do right at this second?"

"Don't you?" Néron asked.

"Get in there and take the compound," Brenna snarled. "That's an order."

Néron raised an eyebrow at her but did as she said, leaving the shelter of one of the trucks and starting to skirt his way around the fight. Brenna turned her attention back to the compound and surveyed it. No bikes out here, but maybe she could make her way inside and find one. They had to be near the entrance, didn't they? Brenna took a deep breath, steeling herself to leave the safety of the trucks' blockade. She looked around and realized she was the only Eagle left, everyone else had already run out into the fight. Brenna lay down on her belly in the dirt and looked under one of the trucks out towards the melee. There were more Slavers on the ground than Eagles, but she knew they had a population advantage. God only knew how many were inside, waiting to come out. Plus they had the advantage of using slaves as cannon fodder if they had to. Brenna returned to her feet and prepared herself. Get inside, find a bike, find the bitch. The less complicated the plan, the more effective it was likely to be. For the first time in a couple days, Brenna smiled. This was going to work.

36

THE SCOUT FELT heavier with every step Scarlett took, and Scarlett kept a running stream of curse words flowing through her head. Some of the scout's wounds reopened and Scarlett could feel the blood smearing as she carried the unconscious woman. Scarlett wondered if when she found some clothes, she could find something to wrap around the scout, hopefully to keep the wounds closed or, at the very least, keep her from bleeding all over Scarlett. Scarlett rather liked the name she'd chosen for herself, but she wasn't interested in showing that by wearing someone else's blood. Frankly, the idea of it grossed her out a little, but Scarlett tried not to think about it despite the coppery metallic smell that filled her nose. Then again, after everything she'd been through over the last few days, having someone bleed on her seemed like the least of her worries.

Scarlett reached the corner of the building and stopped. She considered setting down the scout and running inside herself, but Scarlett didn't want to risk the Slavers finding her. If the scout was going to bleed all over her, it wasn't going to be for nothing. Scarlett peeked around the edge of the building, checking for people, but there was still no one. She set down the rifle for a moment, leaning it against the building as she readjusted her hold on the scout. The scout groaned slightly.

"Oh good, you're not dead," Scarlett said as she picked up the rifle once more. The scout said nothing, lapsing back into unconsciousness.

Scarlett turned the corner just as a Slaver pushed open the building's front door.

"Hey," the Slaver said, taking a second to register the sight of Scarlett carrying a bloody and beaten scout. But a second was all she needed and Scarlett lifted the rifle and shot him in the forehead. The Slaver went down and Scarlett stepped daintily over him to get to the door. Scout blood on her, that she'd come to accept. Stepping in Slaver blood? No, thank you. All of the Slavers smelled disgusting, and Scarlett wondered if bathing was a regular part of their tribal customs. She seriously doubted it.

Inside the building, Scarlett quickly scanned the area, looking for stairs. Where the fuck were the stairs? There, just down the hall to her left. Duh. Scarlett moved quickly, tightening her grip on the scout to keep her from slipping off her shoulder. Then she heard the sound of approaching footsteps descending the stairs. *Shit.* Knowing she had to act quickly, she grabbed the first door handle she could reach, praying it wasn't locked and that the room wasn't occupied. Lucky for her, both of her wishes were granted. Scarlett carried the scout inside as fast as she could and shut the door silently, holding the handle all the way to the side to keep it from clicking. Scarlett released it slowly, bit by bit. Once that was done, she exhaled. Scarlett turned to face the room and saw a couple of chairs and a cabinet. She used her free hand and one of her feet to line up the chairs to create a sort of bench and gently laid the scout down across them. The scout moaned softly, but didn't wake up. Scarlett sighed and put her hands on her hips as she stared down at the scout.

"What the fuck am I supposed to do with you?" Scarlett asked. She knew she couldn't leave her with the Slavers, that much was evident. Actually, Scarlett wasn't sure why she'd taken her in the first place. This scout had been nothing but a giant pain in the ass, and yet Scarlett couldn't just leave her to die some horrible, torturous, slow death at the hands of these psychopaths.

"God dammit," Scarlett muttered.

She turned to survey the room once more and her eyes landed on the cabinet. *Please be a closet, please be a closet, please be a closet* Scarlett chanted silently as she walked to the cabinet. She pulled it open and it was empty, save for one folded white sheet. Scarlett figured the cabinet must be some kind of linen closet, but, really, she didn't give a fuck what it was used for. The sight of fabric was such a relief. Scarlett pulled out the folded sheet and held it to her face, breathing in its clean smell. The Slavers might not bathe themselves, but it seemed they at least washed their linens. Scarlett unfolded it, letting the sheet tumble open in front of her and she held it up to her body, trying to figure out the best way to tie it around herself to make some sort of toga or wrap dress. Practical? Not really, but Scarlett was so thrilled to have fabric against her body that she would've worn a ball gown if that was available.

As Scarlett began to wrap herself in the sheet, her eyes fell on the scout and Scarlett stopped as she watched some of the cuts on the scout's arm ooze blood. Scarlett glanced back in the cabinet to confirm that this was the only sheet before looking down at the fabric in her hands. Scarlett stamped her foot, feeling completely pissed off, but she took the sheet from her body and laid it out on the floor. Then she gently picked up the scout and laid her down on the sheet before she wrapped it around her. Okay, this was okay. Scarlett could deal with this. The sheet could help stop the scout's blood flow and if that stupid Slaver had been telling the truth, all Scarlett had to do was get upstairs to find some clothes. She could probably even leave the scout here while she got clothes and then pick her up on the way out. Yes, that would work. Scarlett picked up the rifle and just as her fingertips touched the cool metal of the doorknob, an explosion rocked the building.

"What the fuck?!" Scarlett exclaimed before clapping a hand over her mouth. *Brilliant job, idiot, why don't you just open the door and yell for the Slavers to come find you?* She closed her eyes for a moment, disappointment and anger pulsing through her veins, but she knew they had to get out. She picked up the scout, wrapped like a mummy, and hoisted her over her shoulder. Scarlett opened the door and immediately saw three Slavers jogging towards the front entrance. She shot them all in quick succession and stepped out into the hallway. Scarlett hesitated as she looked longingly towards the stairs. *Fuck*. Oh well. She figured she'd gone for this long without clothes, what was a little longer?

"God fucking dammit," Scarlett said as she turned towards the front door of the building and carried the scout outside.

37

GRUN SAT FORWARD in his chair, his hands knotted in front of him. He was alone in the inner sanctum with The Pet who stood by the door, alert as always. Grun examined her from where she stood, letting his eyes run up from her scuffed black boots, over her nude body, and up to her helmet. She wore it so often that at times, Grun found himself forgetting what her face looked like under there. But he preferred her to wear the helmet, especially in public. People found it unnerving and he wanted to keep them as uncomfortable as possible. Grun let his eyes fall back down to her hands, neatly folded in front of her and still smeared with the scout's blood. Sometimes he wondered if he should add gloves to her outfit to help protect her hands, but he wasn't sure if it would add to or detract from the reputation he'd cultivated for her. This, however, convinced him that he'd been right to hold off on the gloves. The red streaks created a gloved effect anyway, and all of the Slavers who had been in the arena knew where that blood had come from. By refusing to let her wash her hands, Grun was encouraging her image as something primal, something unpredictable. A beast doesn't brush its teeth after shredding a bunny rabbit; therefore, neither would The Pet.

Grun pulled his eyes away from The Pet and looked at his own hands. They were shaking a little and he gripped them tighter, lacing his fingers like a corset until his knuckles turned white. He knew an uprising was forming. He'd heard more whispers while he'd walked amongst the Slavers as he headed back towards the inner sanctum after leaving the arena. Grun hadn't been able to pinpoint who said what, but that almost made it more ominous. He didn't want to be paranoid, but this was real. This was a war. And this was how he himself had ascended to power.

Grun sat back in his chair, still looking at his hands. The best way to deal with this would be to win this battle as quickly as possible. Take down the Eagle leaders, take the rest of them as prisoners. At least, he'd keep the women. Realistically speaking, Grun knew that the best way to get the Eagle leaders would be to send The Pet after them, but that option made him nervous. With things being as tenuous as they were with the loyalty of his people, he was hesitant to let The Pet leave his sight. But faster was better. He didn't want to give the Slavers even more opportunities to plot against him. Get the Eagles, keep control. Grun could go after the Eagle leaders himself, but The Pet was faster, more efficient. He looked back at her, taut and ready to spring at any moment. Yes, the blood on her hands was the right touch to complete her battle look.

"Come here," Grun said softly, beckoning to The Pet.

She walked over obediently and Grun patted his knee gently. She stared at it, uncomprehending.

"Sit down," he said.

She sat down, her posture perfect. The way he'd taught her. Grun reached up and slowly removed her helmet, pulling it back to reveal her face. Her head was shaved, but the hair had begun to grow back in. Grun ran a hand over her scalp and the velvety fuzz reminded him a little of a puppy. He let his gaze wander down her face, taking in the scars and burns stitched across what would have been an otherwise beautiful face. His fingers gently traced a line of rumpled skin that ran down the length of her cheek. Grun leaned closer to her, his lips only an inch away from hers, when he looked into her eyes. Her eyes were gray and flat, awaiting instruction. Grun stopped and leaned back in his chair. He stared at her for a long time as she sat, unmoving, on his knee. He felt disappointed as he looked at her, although he couldn't quite articulate why. The Pet was everything he wanted, everything he'd worked for. The perfect creation. Grun cleared his throat.

"Go back to your post," he said, not unkindly, as he replaced the helmet over her head. She stood and he quickly slapped her across the rear, the smack of skin on skin contact loud in the inner sanctum. The Pet did as he said and crossed the room to resume her position, bloodied hands folded in front of her once more.

Suddenly, the room shook. Grun released his hands and gripped the arms of his chair. Even The Pet stumbled, quickly regaining her balance before she looked towards him.

"What the fuck was that?" Grun asked.

The Pet said nothing, awaiting instructions. Grun stood up and quickly crossed the room to the door. He unlocked it and yanked it open to see a few Slavers in the outer sanctum climbing back to their feet.

"What happened?" Grun demanded as another Slaver jogged into the room.

"Eagle bomb," the Slaver said, panting. "A few have made it into the compound."

"Well, then get them out!" Grun roared. "Why the fuck didn't anyone tell me they were here yet?!"

"Grand Master, they just—"

"They just *nothing*! Eagles arrive, someone informs me. That's the way it works. I shouldn't have to wait to hear about it until they're blowing shit up, and I'm not interested in your fucking excuses," Grun snarled. Behind him, The Pet stepped up to stand at his elbow, sliding her rifle around from her back to her front. The messenger Slaver took a step back.

"Well?" Grun asked impatiently.

"They . . . they're here," the messenger Slaver stammered.

"Well, then, I guess we have a war to fight," Grun said. "Get the fuck out there."

The Slavers in the room all hurried out, one nearly tripping over his own feet before catching himself on the door frame. Grun watched them leave and rolled his eyes. Fuck, he better be able to maintain control because if he ended up having to serve one of those idiots, he'd kill himself and save them the trouble.

Grun motioned to The Pet and they followed the other Slavers and made their way out from the lower level of the building up to the main floor. Part of a wall was blown out and Grun and The Pet had to step their way over the rubble in order to exit the building. Grun pulled his gun and surveyed the scene in front of him. There were several dead bodies nearby, both Slaver and Eagle, and the compound was in chaos. Grun took a deep breath. This was it.

"Find the Eagle leaders and kill them immediately. When you're done, find me."

The Pet nodded and jogged away, turning her head this way and that to locate her targets. She rounded a corner and left Grun's sight, leaving him alone. Now, as long as nobody shot him until she returned, he'd be fine.

Right?

Grun kept his gun level and ready as he moved through the compound, watching for the slightest hint of a feather. Then he saw something that made him pause. Up ahead, there was a naked woman with dark hair and a rifle in her hand. That alone wouldn't have been particularly interesting at that moment, except for what the woman had over her shoulder. There, wrapped in a bloodstained sheet, was the scout from the arena.

"Motherfucker!" Grun exclaimed. And then the ground in front of him exploded.

38

WHEN SCARLETT EMERGED from the building with the scout, there was a flurry of activity that hadn't been there when she'd entered the building.

"Of fucking course," Scarlett groaned as she saw the Slavers running along the footpaths. One turned to see her and opened his mouth to shout. Before he could make a sound, Scarlett shot him and three more Slavers. *Fuck, how many bullets does this magazine hold? Should've counted. Should've done a lot of things. I'll just add it to the list.* Scarlett kept moving forward and two of the feather people rounded the corner. One of them raised his gun at her so she took out both of them, red flowers blooming across their shirts and vining over their woven leather armor. She hurried forward and heard someone yell behind her just before an explosion rocked the ground, causing her to stumble to her knees. The scout fell from her shoulder and landed hard on the ground.

"Owww," the scout moaned. "Tha' hurrr."

"You know what, princess? It's a little hard to carry a sack of fucking potatoes when shit is exploding," Scarlett hissed. She put her weight on one foot, then the other. Scarlett reached down and brushed the dirt and rocks from her kneecaps. Fuck, that hurt. How was it that those stupid little rocks hurt the worst? Well, Scarlett reconsidered, maybe not the worst. She was pretty sure the kid whose knee she'd blown open would beg to differ.

"Don' be meeeeean," the scout whined, her jaw swollen.

"We'll have to compromise and have an etiquette lesson lesson later when no one is trying to murder us," Scarlett said as she slung the scout back over her shoulder.

"Okaaaaaay," the scout said, her voice sleepy and fading quickly.

"It's a deal," Scarlett said as she picked the rifle back up. There were some men on the ground behind her, probably knocked down or injured by the latest explosion, but they would be up on their feet soon. She had to move.

Scarlett tried to resume her previous pace but she found her left knee to be a little sore from the fall. *Excellent, that's exactly what I need. I need to fuck up one of my major joints so that I turn into a sitting fucking duck in the middle of some fucking battle when all I want is some fucking pants.* Scarlett glanced at the red stained sheet wrapped around the scout. Never in her life had she been so jealous over a bed sheet. As she hurried around the compound, shooting the occasional Slaver, and despite the adrenaline pumping through her, Scarlett found her thoughts wandering from the bed sheet to a bed. A real bed. God, it felt forever since she'd slept in a real bed. She and Mel had spent a lot of time on the road, but even then, there were taverns along the way with rooms to rent. Some were better than others, but all had at least had a bed and a pillow. To be fair, "pillow" seemed at times to be a somewhat loose term to some of the tavern owners. Once, Scarlett and Mel had stayed at one place that had offered pillows that had nearly been completely deflated. Many of the feathers had been forced out of weak seams and those that were left seemed to have completely given up on life. At the time, Scarlett had felt annoyed and had spent a restless night tossing and turning, using her arms in place of a pillow until they went numb. Now, she wished she could go back in time and punch herself in the face. Scarlett would have loved to have a deflated pillow during any of the times she'd managed to grab hold of a few minutes of sleep during the past few days. She wondered where Mel was and what sort of bedding she was probably taking for granted. Thinking of Mel made Scarlett mad all over again, but the anger pushed her forward a little faster. *I'm going to get out of here and then I'm going to find you, you bitch.*

Scarlett reached what looked like the entrance to the compound and took out one more Slaver who had been blocking her exit. She peeked out of the opening and saw a battle raging between Slavers and the feather people. God fucking dammit, she was so sick of ending up in the middle of this fucking fight. They could completely wipe each other out for all she fucking cared, she just wanted to leave and find a pair of shoes. Scarlett surveyed the scene in front of her. From what she could tell, most of the fighting seemed to be happening in front of her and within the compound. If she could get out and around to the side, maybe she could regroup for a second and figure out what to do next. Yes, that'd have to do.

Scarlett stepped out from behind the compound entrance and moved as fast as her body would allow while carrying the increasingly heavy scout. Several Slavers turned towards her and raised their guns, but Scarlett took each of them out, one handed and on the move. *Sorry, fellas, I don't have time for your shit.* She noticed a few of the feather people hesitate when they saw her shoot the Slavers, watching her in surprise. Scarlett was prepared to take them out as well, but the feather people didn't raise their rifles in her direction. *You don't shoot me, I won't shoot you* Scarlett thought. After waking up hogtied in the back of a truck, she wasn't exactly a fan of the feather people, but she preferred to save her ammo if she could; she had no idea when she'd be able to grab a bullet refill. Scarlett managed to make it to the edge of the building and had just turned the corner when a hand closed around her arm.

39

SCARLETT WHIRLED AROUND, the scout over her shoulder nearly throwing her off balance, and shoved the barrel of her rifle into the gut of the person who'd grabbed her arm. She was about to pull the trigger when she flicked her eyes up to the person's face and she saw Néron looking back at her.

"Holy shit, Néron!" Scarlett exclaimed.

"I still don't appreciate that kind of language," Néron said firmly, setting his mouth in a hard, dissatisfied line.

"Well, excuse me, but I nearly shot you because you snuck up on me. Which do you prefer, bad language or a bullet to the stomach?" Scarlett retorted petulantly.

Néron glared at her, but didn't answer her question.

"What are you doing here?" he asked. Néron glanced at the bundle on Scarlett's shoulder. "Is she dead?"

"No, unfortunately. And I don't know why I'm here, I'm just trying to get the fuck out," Scarlett said.

"Oops, sorry," she said when she noticed Néron's brow furrow disapprovingly.

Néron grunted.

"Look, I found her all fu—beaten up and she was going to die if she stayed there, so I had to get her out," Scarlett said, catching her language just in time.

Néron surveyed the blood seeping through the bed sheet and nodded.

"Come on," he said, motioning for her to follow.

"Where?" Scarlett asked suspiciously. She looked to the side and saw a Slaver lining up a shot at Néron. Scarlett fired off a bullet and the Slaver hit the ground with one less eye.

"Do you really have time to debate this?" Néron asked, exasperated.

"The last time I went anywhere with you I ended up hogtied in the back of a truck!" Scarlett protested.

Néron shrugged.

"I'm out of rope. Are you coming?"

A bullet whizzed over the top of Scarlett's head and she turned and fired a shot at another Slaver, hitting him squarely in the belly.

"God, fine, yes, I'm coming," she said.

Scarlett followed Néron around the edge of the battlefield, trying to keep the scout from bouncing too much as she ran. Néron led her towards the grouping of Eagle trucks and Scarlett ran hard as they got closer. *So close. Come on. Run faster, you idiot* she scolded herself. Just short of the trucks, Scarlett's foot hit a dip in the ground and she crashed forward, landing hard on the ground. The scout hit the ground beside her with a sickening thump.

"Fuck!" Scarlett shouted.

Néron leaned out from behind a truck and glared at her before he grabbed the scout by the bedsheet and dragged her to shelter. Scarlett followed, scrabbling across the ground and dragging the rifle with her.

"I can put her in the back of one of the trucks," Néron said. "We'll lay her down and kind of slide her under the bench and then we can even put some supply packs in front of her to kind of hide her. Will that work?"

"Yeah," Scarlett said. She looked down at the scout's bruised, swollen face. "Thanks."

A barrage of bullets hit the front of the truck.

"Shit," Scarlett said. When Néron glared at her, she rolled her eyes. "Oh, come on, I can't even swear if someone is shooting at me?" He said nothing. "That's some bullshit right there," Scarlett muttered. "Okay, here's the deal, you get her in the truck, I'll pull the Slavers away."

"What?" Néron asked. "No. You can't take on that many by yourself."

"Tell you what, if you're wrong, I'll never swear again," Scarlett said sweetly, batting her eyes at him before she pulled the nearly full clip from his rifle and attached it to her own. Without waiting for his reply, Scarlett stood up and walked out from behind the truck, raising the rifle to her shoulder.

"You fuckers are in trouble now," Scarlett muttered as the Slavers descended upon her. "And someone is going to give me a fucking shirt."

40

SCARLETT WAS A blur of dark hair and slightly sunburned flesh, firing bullets and using the rifle as a club to break noses, arms, and legs, seemingly all at the same time. Néron watched her from behind the truck as she seemed to move further and further away with each kill, drawing the Slavers away from the trucks and into her tornadic path of destruction. He'd never seen anyone fight quite like that before. Néron sighed. She'd never stop swearing now.

Néron picked up the wrapped scout and laid her in the back of the truck as gently as he could before he jumped up beside her. He eased her underneath the bench and grabbed the spare supply bags, shielding her from view. She groaned slightly, painfully, but didn't wake. Néron reached into one of the supply packs and pulled out a new magazine and clipped it into his rifle. He glanced back at Scarlett and saw that her attackers' numbers had fallen significantly, but there were more on the way. Néron raised his rifle to his shoulder, but a bullet tore through his bicep. He yelled in pain through gritted teeth and dropped out of sight down into the bed of the truck. Lying on his back, Néron clapped a hand over the wound, applying pressure as blood seeped through his fingers. He turned his head to the side and noticed his face was level with the unconscious scout's. Part of him wanted to keep lying there, just hide in the truck for a while, but he pushed himself to his knees and used his knife to cut off a strip of fabric from the scout's bedsheet.

"Sorry," Néron apologized. "I just need a little. I'll pay you back." He wrapped the fabric around his arm as a tourniquet and sat back for a moment, breathing hard through the pain. It was time to get back out there.

Scarlett looked around, surveying the battle. Christ, she did not want to fucking be here. She really didn't give a fuck if these people all killed each other, she just wanted to get out and find some fucking pants. Was that too much to ask? *Apparently* Scarlett thought bitterly as she felled a few more Slavers, rather enjoying the rapid *pop-pop-pop* of the rifle in spite of herself. The familiar sound was comforting and Scarlett felt more like herself than she had in days, at least since she had woken up in this god forsaken desert.

By the way, Scarlett thought as she executed a clean headshot on a raging Slaver, *fuck you, Mel.*

Scarlett heard the approaching roar of a motorbike and she turned towards the sound. *Oh god, what now?* She squinted, trying to see the identity of the rider, and was surprised to see it was an Eagle, not a Slaver. None of the other Eagles seemed to have bikes, why did this one? As the bike drew closer, Scarlett recognized the woman driving it and groaned. The woman's face was contorted with rage as she yelled, charging straight at Scarlett.

"Really, bitch?" Scarlett yelled at Brenna over the sound of the motorbike.

Brenna screamed again with rage. Scarlett picked up the rifle and fired at the shoulder joint of Brenna's armor. Her shot hit its target and Brenna flew backwards off the bike, which sped forward without her for several yards before toppling onto its side.

"You fucking shot me?!" Brenna screamed at Scarlett.

"Yeah, I fucking shot you!" Scarlett yelled as she walked towards her. "You were going to run me over!"

"You had it coming, you thieving bitch," Brenna snarled as she swiped an ineffective hand out towards Scarlett's ankles. Scarlett easily stepped back out of reach.

"We're still on that? Christ, you're annoying," Scarlett said.

"You need to pay for what you took from me," Brenna said.

"Whatever," Scarlett said, firing a shot into Brenna's thigh. Brenna screamed and writhed on the ground as Scarlett reached down and unclipped the magazine from Brenna's gun. Then she turned and jogged towards the fallen motorbike, hoping this one would last longer than the other one she'd borrowed.

41

THE PET MOVED in the shadows, stalking her prey. The Eagles were up ahead and although they were attentive to their surroundings, none of them noticed she was there until she struck out, slicing their throats. She liked the way the blood spilled over her fingers, like she was squeezing an overripe fruit. The Pet wanted to take the time to rip out their throats and eviscerate their bodies, but she was on a mission. She had a purpose. Find the Eagle leaders, kill them immediately, find her master.

After cutting down a couple captains, the Pet spotted the Eagles' general. Yes. That one. That was the one she needed. The Pet wiped off the blade of her knife with her fingers, flinging off the excess blood. She wiped her hand on her leg, streaking it with warpaint. The Pet moved swiftly, ready to strike like a snake at the woman's neck, when suddenly four men descended on her, each one grabbing a limb as they slammed her to the ground. The Pet twisted violently like a fox caught in a trap, but the men held firm. The one gripping her left arm repeatedly punched the back of her hand until it reflexively opened and the knife dropped from her grasp. The Pet snarled and struggled violently, yanking her limbs, but the four men were too much for her. One of them dropped a loop of rope around her wrist, tightening it like a noose before her arm was wrenched behind her back. Her other arm and legs were similarly captured and pulled back, tied into a neat bouquet of hands and boots. The Pet roared with fury, her voice ringing out across the desert and above the clatter of the battle.

Inside the compound, Grun heard The Pet's furious cry and his stomach dropped. Shit. His hands started to shake. Fuck. He couldn't do that. He didn't know for sure what had happened. Except he did; The Pet never made a noise without a directive. For her to yell like that, it could only mean . . . well, he knew what it meant. Grun gripped the handle of his knife in his belt, willing his hands to be still and regain their composure. It's not over yet. It's not over. He glanced around himself at the other Slavers rushing out of the compound. No one else had seemed to notice or respond to The Pet's roar. Then Grun realized none of them had ever heard her voice. For all they knew, that was an Eagle. But they wouldn't think that for long. Grun didn't know what he'd see once he exited the compound, but as soon as the Slavers saw The Pet was incapacitated, he was done for.

Grun walked towards the entrance to the compound, trying to keep his composure. *Don't walk too fast, don't let them see your fear. Maintain control.* When he reached the entrance, he immediately searched the landscape for The Pet. At first, he couldn't find her amidst the broken bodies that lay splayed out on the dirt. It wasn't lost on him that there were vastly more Slavers than Eagles on the ground. Shots were flying and the angry, warring shouts of battle filled the air, pulling at his attention, but then he saw The Pet. Hogtied and carried by four Eagles, she thrashed and screamed and fought as they carried her towards their trucks, but to no avail; they had her. It couldn't end like this. It wouldn't end like this. Grun's fear turned over into anger and the sight of The Pet captured by the Eagles enraged him. If he was going to do something, he had to do it fast.

And then he saw someone else.

Near the grouping of Eagle vehicles, Grun saw a naked woman with a rifle, picking off Slavers like petals off a flower. That fucking bitch. That was the one that took the scout. That fucking cunt. Grun's angry breathing swelled in him, flooding his vision with hate. He turned back just inside the compound's entrance to the motorbike yard. The lock had been shot off of the fencing, but Grun didn't care. He grabbed the first bike he could reach and sat on it, revving the engine, fueling his anger. Grun walked the bike out of the yard and headed for the entrance. He pulled out of the compound just as the naked woman shot an Eagle in the leg. Grun watched as the woman took something from the Eagle before she jogged towards a fallen motorbike.

I don't think so, bitch Grun thought as he began to accelerate the bike. *I don't fucking think so*.

As the bike approached, one of the Slavers reached out a hand from where he lay on the ground.

Roan. Grun swerved the bike and ran over Roan's hand. Roan yelled, his profanities lost in the sound of the motorbike's engine. Grun smiled a little. *That's what you get for staging a coup, you little shit.* Up ahead, that naked bitch had righted the bike and started it, pulling away from the battle. Determined, Grun pushed the bike faster. He'd get her. He knew he would.

42

As Scarlett rode the motorbike away from the fight, she let herself enjoy the feel of the wind in her face. It was the freest she'd felt in days and she wanted to revel in the sensation, if only for a little while. She closed her eyes, absorbed in the moment, and, without realizing it, released the gas a little on the bike. *Oh my god, you fucking idiot, escape the desert psychos and THEN relax*. Scarlett opened her eyes and was about to accelerate again when something slammed into the back of her bike and she went flying, tumbling head over heels over the handlebars of the bike. The motorbike itself fell on its side and the momentum made it spin haphazardly across the dirt. Scarlett landed hard on the ground, flat on her back, as she stared up at the blue, cloudless sky.

"What. The. Fuck," Scarlett wheezed, trying to regain the wind that had been knocked out of her. Had she hit a rock? No, something had definitely hit her. Nothing had exploded, so it couldn't have been a missile. Scarlett gingerly lifted her head and propped herself up on her elbows. A tiny rock dug into her left elbow and she winced. *Fuck rocks*.

Scarlett scanned the area and she saw not one bike, but two. Near the second one was a large man, a Slaver by the look of his clothes, his head bald and shining in the hot desert sun, who was attempting to get back on his feet.

"Did you just fucking run into me?" Scarlett demanded as she stood up. "On *purpose*? What is your fucking problem?"

The man raised his head and looked at her, his eyes narrowing at the sight of her.

"You fucking cunt," he growled. "Taking what doesn't belong to you."

"Oh my god, this again? What, are you friends with that feather lady?" Scarlett asked. Jesus Christ, she was so fucking done with these people. "Look, I'm sorry I took the bike. Actually, no, I'm not that sorry. I just want to get the fuck out of here."

"Not the bike," Grun said, standing up to his full height. "The girl."

"What girl?" Scarlett asked, confused. Then she remembered the scout. "You mean the woman I found beaten half to death?"

"She wasn't yours to take!" Grun screamed at her. About 100 yards away, Scarlett could see feather people congregating near the trucks. A few of them seemed to be carrying a mostly naked woman who was hogtied but thrashing violently. *Fight all you want, honey, they're really good at those knots.*

"She's not yours to own," Scarlett said, looking back at Grun. "She's a person, not a thing." She unhooked the rifle from her back and held it in front of her, aiming at Grun's forehead.

"She is whatever I say she is," Grun snarled. "Do you know what you've done? Do you know the kind of damage you've caused?"

"The damage *I've* caused?" Scarlett said, her voice rising. "Are you fucking kidding me? Do you have any idea what *I* have had to put up with? I'm not running around here naked because I enjoy third degree sunburns. I was dumped naked into this god forsaken desert by my partner, I was shot at by goons that look like you, and acquired a pretty ineffective stalker who was too fucked up to even know where she was half the time. *Then* I was captured by these fucking feather people and this psycho woman developed an obsession over me. Then I got caught in a firefight between two tribes, who can blow each other the fuck up for all I care. I managed to get away and ended up spending a night in a tree while a giant beast tried to figure out the best way to eat me. After that, I nearly drowned in some underground waterway, and, lucky me, ended up in your goddamn building. Then, apparently, your stupid fucking war is still going on and I was attacked by idiots that look like you and that obsessed psycho bitch with the feathers, only to think I was finally getting away from all of you, and then you crashed into me," Scarlett yelled, jabbing the rifle towards Grun. "And I've had to do all of this without so much as a *FUCKING PAIR OF SOCKS*."

Grun glared at her and took a step forward. Scarlett fired the rifle. But instead of shooting a bullet, the rifle gave a polite click. Empty. Grun paused, staring at the rifle. When he realized what the click meant, he lunged for Scarlett. Scarlett quickly flipped the rifle and swung it like a bat. The butt of the gun connected with his ear and Grun howled. He grabbed the rifle before she could swing it again and while his hands were occupied, Scarlett delivered a swift kick to his knee. Grun's knee nearly buckled, but he stayed on his feet. Enraged, he wrenched the rifle away from Scarlett and threw it aside. The gun clattered as it hit the dry ground. Scarlett jabbed up at Grun's windpipe but he leaned back, lessening the impact. Grun swept Scarlett's feet and she fell back on the ground, pain singing in her elbows and tailbone. He picked up his boot to stomp on her head, but Scarlett rolled away, jumping to her feet.

"Go ahead, keep it up," Grun said, breathing hard. "This will only make it more fun when I rip out your fucking throat."

"That's sweet of you, but I really prefer that my throat stays where it is," Scarlett replied.

Grun lunged at her again and she stepped to meet him, shoving her knee into his groin. Grun groaned and fell to the ground. He dry heaved as Scarlett scanned the area. Gun, gun, where was the gun? Scarlett saw it out past Grun so she leaped over him, clearing his bulk, but he grabbed her ankle, yanking her down to the ground. Grun kept a vice grip on her leg, pulling himself over to her. Scarlett tried to kick him with her free foot, but he sat on her thighs, pinning them down. He grabbed her throat with both hands and started to squeeze. Scarlett pulled at his fingers, trying to pry them up, but they were strong and steadfast. He pushed harder, and Scarlett knew she only had one chance to stay alive. Her vision started to blacken around the edges and she violently stabbed her fingers at Grun's eyes. She felt one of them give way under two of her fingers and Grun screamed, momentarily loosening his grip. That moment was all she needed and Scarlett summoned all of her strength and heaved him off of her, shoving him to the side. Blood poured down his face and Scarlett took her chance, leaping on top of him as she began to punch him as hard as she could in his face. His nose shattered under the second punch and Grun clawed at her, trying to throw her off, but Scarlett locked her knees around his chest, never once slowing her punching. His face was bloody and slowly kneading into a pulpy mess under her blows. Scarlett felt her knuckles split on a piece of his exposed cheekbone, but she kept hitting and hitting and hitting.

"Fuck! All of you! I just! Want! Some fucking! Clothes!" Scarlett yelled with each punch.

Grun's hands grew weak and then stopped moving completely, his arms falling outspread on the ground. It took Scarlett a moment to notice that he'd stopped fighting and another to stop punching. Grun's face was soaked in blood and unrecognizable. Scarlett slowly got to her feet and took a few steps away from his body, just in case he grabbed for her again. However, it seemed unlikely he was going to grab anybody anytime soon. Scarlett looked down at her hand, covered in blood, and flicked her hand to the side, flinging off the blood like errant water droplets. Then she turned and saw that the feather people had come closer, evidently to get a better seat for the show. Dangling from a cord around one of their necks, Scarlett saw a single red feather, vibrant as the blood on her hand.

"Fucking feathers," Scarlett said. Then she blacked out.

43

WHEN SCARLETT'S EYES fluttered open, she felt certain she was dead.

There's no other explanation. After everything, I finally fucking died.

It then occurred to her that if she was thinking thoughts like that, she probably wasn't dead. Then again, she'd never died before, so who the fuck knew what one could or couldn't do while dead? Scarlett opened her eyes all the way and looked around. The room was clean and white with a few empty beds on either side of her, illuminated by glowing lanterns on the walls. Scarlett looked down at herself and realized she was in a bed.

"Holy shit," Scarlett said in disbelief, running her hands over the sheet. She reached back and touched the pillow, luxuriating in the feel of having something soft behind her head. God, she'd almost forgotten what a pillow felt like. When Scarlett brought her hand back down to rest on top of the sheet, she noticed there was a tube hooked up to the back of it. Her eyes followed the tube and saw it was connected to a bag of clear liquid, hanging from a hook by her bed. Like a hospital? Was she in a hospital? Scarlett looked around again and supposed that would explain the row of beds. *Duh, idiot.* Scarlett looked down at her front and realized she was still naked. *Oh, god dammit.* Although, she supposed having a sheet was better than nothing. True, she would've preferred pants and a shirt and maybe a pair of boots, but a sheet was far more than she'd had for the past few days.

Wait, how had she gotten to the hospital? Where even was this hospital? Who was running it? Scarlett tried to think of the last thing she could remember before waking up here. She'd gone swimming and come up through the floor. Someone must have found her and brought her to a hospital wing. Scarlett picked up her head and looked down at her free hand, the one not hooked up to the IV, and saw a bandage wrapped around it. She tried to flex her hand within the bandage and her knuckles loudly and painfully protested. No, something else had happened after she'd come up through the floor. Had she been in a fight? She must have been in a fight. Nothing else really seemed to be hurt aside from a general soreness in her limbs. Scarlett flopped her head back against the pillow and pulled the sheet up a little higher. God, she just wanted to wrap herself in it like a cocoon and never come out. A memory tugged at her thoughts. Someone wrapped in a sheet. Was it her? No, it had been someone else. That girl, the one from the shed by the pond.

Suddenly, the memories flooded her brain and she remembered all of it. Scarlett remembered retrieving the scout from the arena and wrapping her in a sheet.

She remembered hiding her in the back of that truck and killing a bunch of those Slavers. She remembered wiping out on a motorbike and getting into a fight with that huge guy. *Right* Scarlett thought, wiggling the fingers of her bandaged hand. *Don't know how I blocked that out*. Then she saw the feathers and . . . oh no. Christ, she'd probably been brought here to get justice for shooting that feather lady in the leg. Seriously? Was she going to have to fight her way out of another fucking compound? Then again, it seemed a little ridiculous for them to heal her just to punish her. And it's not like she was tied down. But then . . . why was she here?

Scarlett heard approaching footsteps and immediately rolled out of the bed, hitting the tile floor hard. Pain shot up through her injured hand and the other one had a sudden sting in it. Scarlett noticed the IV, half pulled out of her hand, and she removed it all the way, tossing the end up on the bed. The needle flicked stray blood droplets across the white sheet like tiny flowers in the snow. Scarlett crouched behind the bed, which offered almost no protection, but it was better than lying down and waiting for someone to come along and find her incapacitated.

A young woman with dark hair entered the room carrying some folded clothes and a pair of boots. She looked momentarily confused at the sight of the empty bed before she noticed Scarlett behind it.

"Are you okay?" the woman asked, bending down a little in an attempt to meet Scarlett's eyes. "Did you fall?"

"Where am I? Scarlett demanded. "Who are you?"

"Specifically, you're in the hospital wing. Generally speaking, you're at Eagles' Pass," she said. "And I'm Reseda. I'm a healer for the Eagles."

Scarlett stood up slowly.

"How are you feeling?" Reseda asked.

"Okay," Scarlett said tentatively.

"Do you mind if I take a look at your hand?" Reseda asked, pointing to Scarlett's bandage.

"Sure," Scarlett said, sitting down on the bed as cautiously as if it were loaded with explosives.

Reseda set down the clothes and boots on a nearby bed and walked over to Scarlett, who held out her hand. Reseda slowly unwrapped it the bandage.

"You know, you're turning into somewhat of a legend around here," Reseda said.

"What?"

"I didn't see it myself, of course, but everyone was talking about it when they came back," Reseda said as she removed the last of the bandages.

"Talking about what?" Scarlett asked, wincing as Reseda gently examined her hand.

"The way you shot down an entire Slaver army with only one hand on your rifle, the way you killed a man four times your size with your bare hands," Reseda said. "Plus, that doesn't even include what you survived from a medical standpoint. I tested your blood when you came in here, and you had an incredibly toxic cocktail of drugs in your system. The fact that you were able to fight, let alone open your eyes, is nothing short of incredible," Reseda added as she reached for a fresh roll of bandages.

"My partner drugged me and dumped me in the desert," Scarlett said quietly.

"Ex-partner, I hope," Reseda replied. Scarlett thought of Mel, but then pushed her away quickly. "Your hand looks pretty good," Reseda said, winding a new bandage around it and securing it tightly. "I brought you some clothes," she added, pointing to the nearby bed. "If you'll get dressed, the Elders want to see you."

"The Elders?" Scarlett asked.

"Yes," Reseda said. "I'll wait for you in the hall."

Reseda left the room, leaving Scarlett alone with the clothes and her thoughts. She couldn't for the life of her figure out what the Elders would want with her. Scarlett was, however, quite pleased to see the clothes. She eased herself to the floor and walked over to the other bed. The top was fitted, with buttons down the front, and the pants were brown. Scarlett was surprised to find that everything fit, especially the boots, but then she figured someone must have measured her while she was unconscious. She knelt down to lace the boots and reveled in the way the leather wrapped around her foot. Scarlett stood up again and straightened the shirt. It was funny—after days of wanting nothing more than to wear clothes, her body felt strange and constricted now that she finally had them. Oh well. She'd get over it soon enough.

Scarlett took a deep breath and headed out into the hallway to meet Reseda. At least the Elders were one set of people she'd be able to meet without her ass hanging out for everyone to see.

44

As Reseda led her through the compound, Scarlett began to feel increasingly uncomfortable. The clothes were fine, she was already readjusting to not being feral, but the stares from the Eagles were a little unnerving. Whenever Scarlett passed, conversation ceased immediately and their eyes fixed on her.

"Why is everyone staring at me?" Scarlett whispered to Reseda.

"I told you," Reseda replied. "You're big news around here. No one in recent memory has killed a Slaver Grand Master with their bare hands."

"A Slaver what?" Scarlett asked.

"Grand Master. The head of the Slavers," Reseda explained. "That's who you were fighting . . . didn't you know?"

Scarlett shook her head.

"Nope. Just thought he was some asshole who crashed into me on a motorbike at the end of a few very shitty days," Scarlett said.

Reseda laughed.

"Well, he could have been that too. He just also happened to be the leader of the Slavers."

Reseda led Scarlett out of the building. The city was nicer than Scarlett had expected, with paved roads and rows of buildings. Very unlike the Slaver compound. Everything was much better maintained, and Scarlett didn't see any half-naked women strung up between two posts and nearly beaten to death, so, all in all, it seemed like an okay place.

Oh, right. Her.

Scarlett had forgotten about the scout. What happened to her? The last she saw her, Néron was going to hide her in a truck. Anything could've happened after that. Scarlett didn't want to dwell on it. She'd gotten the scout out of the compound, she'd done her part. What happened now was up to the scout, assuming she hadn't been blown up or something.

Reseda led Scarlett down the lane to a heavily guarded building. Despite their stoic demeanor, the guards still reacted with amazement when they saw Scarlett, their eyes wide and disbelieving as one of them jumped forward to open the gate.

"This way," Reseda said, motioning for Scarlett to follow her through the gate. Scarlett did so, looking around at the heavily armored guards. Regardless of whether or not they were impressed by her, Scarlett was uncomfortable being unarmed when nearly everyone else around her was. Another guard opened a heavy wooden door and Reseda led Scarlett inside the building.

It took Scarlett's eyes a moment to adjust from the bright sunlight. The room was large and mostly empty, save for a cage at the far end of the room. Inside, a naked woman wearing only boots and a helmet sat on the floor, sulking. Reseda led Scarlett by the cage, and as they passed, the woman in the cage raised her head. Suddenly, the helmeted woman sprang into a furious rage, screaming and straining to reach Scarlett through the bars. Startled, Scarlett leaped back.

"What the fuck?" Scarlett exclaimed, watching as the woman devolved into something primal and decidedly inhuman.

"Oh, her," Reseda said. "She's from the Slaver camp, captured during battle. No one has gotten her to say anything yet. However, this is one of the rare times she's reacted like this. Seems she remembers you."

"I can't imagine why, I have no idea who she is," Scarlett said as The Pet swiped her clawed fingers at Scarlett.

"Maybe she saw you in the battle. You took down a lot of Slavers. Anyway, let's keep going," Reseda said, gesturing for Scarlett to follow her.

Scarlett watched The Pet for another moment, watched her hurl herself against the bars of the cage in futility. Then Scarlett left and followed Reseda, the screams and howls of The Pet echoing off the walls, following her like a shadow.

Reseda led Scarlett down a long hallway and down a short flight of stairs where another guard stood posted. He saw Scarlett and his eyes widened.

"We're here to see the Elders," Reseda said. "This is—"

"I know who this is," the guard said, his eyes still as large as dinner plates. "I wasn't sure you were real, but you are, aren't you?" he asked Scarlett.

"Carver, this really isn't the time," Reseda said at the same time Scarlett asked, "Am I who?"

"The one from the battle! Did you . . ." he started to ask, then hesitated. "I know I shouldn't be asking this, but did you really take out the entire Slaver army by yourself?"

"That's . . . kind of an exaggeration," Scarlett said.

"Did you really kill a bear with your bare hands?" Carver asked.

"I didn't kill it, exactly," Scarlett said. "I'm not even sure it was really a bear. I mean, it kind of looked like a bear, but I can't say for sure . . . wait, how do you even know about that?"

"It's all over the compound, everyone is talking about it," Carver said.

"Okay, this is . . . you know what, whatever," Scarlett said. "Look, I've been summoned, I just want to get this over with so I can get out of here."

"Yes, of course," Carver said, remembering himself and grabbing for the door. "Wait here!" He hurried inside and after a moment, Scarlett heard him loudly announce, "She's here!"

Reseda rolled her eyes.

"Sorry about that," she said to Scarlett.

"Carver, for the last time, you have to stick to protocol when announcing someone," an exasperated voice said from the inside. "I'm not going to tell you again."

"My apologies," Carver said. "Honorable Elders, the—"

"Oh, stop," the voice said. "Just bring her in."

Carver reappeared at the door, poking his flushed face through the opening.

"They're ready for you," he announced.

Scarlett took a step towards the door and glanced over at Reseda.

"Are you coming?" Scarlet asked.

"No, I need to get back," Reseda said. "Besides, they only requested an audience with you."

"Oh," Scarlett said.

"You'll be fine. And if that hand gives you any trouble while you're here, come on back and I'll help you out," Reseda said with a smile.

While I'm here.

"Thanks," Scarlett said. Then she turned and followed Carver through the door.

45

SCARLETT WALKED INTO a large room, illuminated only by the fire pit in the center. Around the fire sat seven people wearing ornate headbands of feathers, watching her with quiet, curious eyes.

I swear to god, if they think I'm going to be some kind of sacrifice, I am going to murder everybody.

One of the women on the opposite side of the fire stood up. She was tall, taller than Scarlett by a good eight inches.

"You are Scarlett," the woman said. A statement, not a question.

"Yes," Scarlett agreed, feeling a little awkward.

"I have heard a lot about you," she said. "The warriors returning from battle have told a lot of stories."

"I think those stories are a little exaggerated," Scarlett said.

"We know what is real and what is not," the woman said, a slight chastising tone in her voice.

"Who are you anyway?" Scarlett asked, surveying the faces of the men and women still seated around the fire.

"We are the Elders of the Eagles," the woman said. "We lead our people in knowledge and wisdom and uphold honor, our highest virtue."

Scarlett nodded, unsure of what else to do.

"I am the High Elder," the woman continued. "I am the head of this council and I have been very interested in speaking with you."

"Okay . . . what do you want to talk about?" Scarlett asked. The room was warm from the fire and Scarlett was beginning to sweat. She was sure that sweat had absolutely nothing to do with the seven creepy people staring at her without blinking.

"From what I understand, you are a fearsome warrior," the High Elder said. She paused, making Scarlett feel the need to fill the silence.

"I've had practice," Scarlett said. *Oh my god, shut up.*

"So I assumed," the High Elder said, her calm and even tone unwavering. She paused again, then continued. "First, I must thank you for defeating the Grand Master. In doing so, you have done a great service for the Eagles and helped us advance our goals of reclaiming our desert."

"You're welcome, but I have to confess, I had no idea who he was," Scarlett said. "I mean, he attacked me, so I fought him. I wasn't trying to do anyone any favors." *Oh my fucking god, what is wrong with you?*

"Whether or not you realized what you were doing does not negate the fact that you did our people a great service," the High Elder said. "The fact that you took on a man so much larger than yourself and managed to beat him with nothing by your hands is impressive."

Scarlett opened her mouth to point out that she'd hit him with the rifle at the beginning of the fight, but thought better of it and closed her mouth.

"Due to your prowess on the battlefield and the service you did for the Eagles, we would like to offer you supplies, weapons, and whatever else you need as well as passage through Eagles' Pass," the High Elder said.

"Thank you," said Scarlett. "Um . . . where exactly is Eagles' Pass?"

"You're here now," the High Elder said, looking amused.

"Yes, but I mean where are we geographically speaking?" Scarlett asked.

"You don't know?"

"No, I was drugged and dumped in the desert," Scarlett explained.

The High Elder smirked, momentarily raising her eyebrows as she considered this information.

"Whoever did that to you clearly had no idea what you are capable of," the High Elder said. "I would not want to be them when you find them."

Scarlett thought of Mel. She wanted to ask the High Elder why she assumed Scarlett was going to go after Mel for vengeance, but stopped herself. Scarlett *was* going to go after Mel. She hadn't fully realized it until that moment, but it was true.

"I will ensure you have a map with your supplies when you leave," the High Elder said. The emphasis on

Scarlett leaving was not lost on her. "Out of curiosity, where were you before you found yourself in Coahuila?"

"A few different places, but mostly Virginia," Scarlett replied.

The High Elder's eyes widened and she smiled again.

"Whoever dropped you here must have been very, very angry with you," she said.

Scarlett's memories before waking up the desert were hazy. She thought she remembered something about someone wanting to kill her, but Mel saying no. Scarlett also vaguely remembered a shiny black scorpion the size of a housecat, so she wasn't entirely sure what was real and what had been a dream.

"An escort will take you to see your friend," the High Elder said, snapping Scarlett out of her own thoughts.

"My friend?" Scarlet asked, her mind still lingering on Mel.

"Yes, the one you brought out of the Slaver compound and hid in our truck. You wrapped her in a sheet," the High Elder clarified.

"Her? Oh, she's not my friend," Scarlett said. "We're not together."

"Your paths are intertwined," the High Elder said. A firm statement that was clearly not open to discussion.

"Look, a few days ago she was stalking me and trying to give me over to the Slavers," Scarlett said. "There's no camaraderie there."

"She was trying to harm you, and yet you saved her from the Slavers instead of leaving her there to die," the High Elder said.

"Well, yeah, but . . . look, she'd been nearly beaten to death by them multiple times, I couldn't just leave here there to die."

"And why not?" asked the High Elder. "As you said, she is not your friend. All she ever did was attempt to cause you harm. Yet you saved her all the same."

"Yes, but . . . I work alone. She's not my problem. I don't care what happens to her now," Scarlett insisted.

"I do not believe that for a moment," the High Elder said. "Your paths are intertwined."

Scarlett thought of protesting again, but instead kept quiet. The High Elder could think whatever she wanted, but Scarlett wasn't going to take that woman with her. End of story.

"An escort is waiting for you outside the door," the High Elder said, gesturing behind Scarlett. "He will get you what you need."

"Okay. Thanks," Scarlett said.

The High Elder nodded and Scarlett turned to leave. When she opened the door, a rush of cool air flowed over her and she felt like she was back in the water, breaking the surface and coming up for air. Another Eagle stood with Carver and he motioned for Scarlett to follow him.

"Bye!" Carver called after her.

Scarlett glanced over her shoulder to see him waving shyly at her. Scarlett's first instinct was to roll her eyes and ignore him, but instead she lifted her hand and offered a small wave in return.

46

THE EAGLE LED Scarlett to a small building nearby. It was another medical room, although not as big or as nice as the one in which Scarlett had woken up. Most of the beds were occupied in this one by Eagle warriors in various states of brokenness from the battle. Scarlett's escort led her to a bed in the back of the room, set a little further away from the others. He brought her to the bed, gave Scarlett a nod, and then turned and left. Scarlett took a breath and faced the hospital bed. The scout looked a lot better than she had the last time Scarlett had seen her. Her body was heavily bandaged, but the swelling in her face had gone down significantly. Other than a particularly gruesome black eye, her face looked almost normal.

"Hey," Scarlett said.

The scout opened her eyes. Her left one was a little swollen from the injury, but she could still open it partway.

"Hi," the scout said.

"So," said Scarlett. "You look better than you did in that arena."

The scout started to laugh but stopped, wincing.

"Yeah," the scout said. "They put some medicine on me and said I should be able to travel tomorrow."

"Where are you going to go?" Scarlett asked, although she was pretty sure she already knew the scout's answer.

"I'm going with you," the scout said automatically.

"I don't think so," Scarlett said. "I'm sorry, I work alone. I have something I need to do, and I can't have anyone tagging along."

"But I have to," the scout said desperately, tears filling the corners of her eyes. "I can't go back to . . . I can't go back."

"Maybe you could stay here," Scarlett said. "You know, help out. Join the Eagles."

The scout shook her head.

"That's not possible. I'm from the Slavers, they'd never let me stay," she said.

"Maybe if you asked them they would," Scarlett offered. "The Elders seem reasonable." Scarlett remembered the High Elder's refrain: *"Your paths are intertwined."*

Shit, there's no way they'd go for that.

The scout shook her head again.

"That's not how it works here," the scout said. "The only reason they didn't leave me to die in the desert is because you carried me out of the compound and they respect you."

Scarlett sighed deeply and looked up at the ceiling. *Fuck.*

"Please, I have nothing left," the scout begged.

Scarlett looked back at her and examined the scout's raw, emotional face. She realized that by saving the scout, she'd taken her on as a responsibility. Christ, think about how brainwashed she'd been, running back to the Slavers who'd beaten the hell out of her. The scout really had nothing left for her here. Scarlett sighed again, a heavy sigh of resignation.

"What's your name?" Scarlett asked.

"I don't have one," the scout said.

"How can you not have a name?" Scarlett asked in disbelief. "Everyone has a name."

"I don't," said the scout.

"What did your masters call you?" Scarlett asked, involuntarily recoiling a little at the word "masters."

"Slave, bitch, cun—" the scout replied, but Scarlett held up a hand to silence her.

"Okay, okay, I get it," Scarlett said. "Well, what do you want your name to be?"

"I don't need one," the scout said.

"Everyone needs a name," Scarlett said. "Mine is Scarlett," she offered.

"Who gave you your name?" asked the scout.

"I did."

"You . . . you chose your own name?" the scout asked.

"Yes," said Scarlett. "You should too."

"I . . . um . . ." the scout said, looking confused and uncertain.

Scarlett shook her head.

"We can work on that later."

"Okay, master," the scout said.

Scarlett put up a hand.

"Not master. Scarlett. I don't own you."

"You . . . what?" the scout asked, confused.

"Maybe we could be . . . friends," Scarlett said slowly, dragging out the word. This scout was not the sort of person she'd ever have chosen for a friend, but it was better than owning her.

"I've never had a friend before," the scout said.

"Never?" Scarlett asked.

The scout shook her head.

"No, I've only ever had my masters," she said.

"You weren't . . . I don't know, friends with any of the other slaves?" Scarlett asked.

"Why would we have been friends?" the scout asked, confused.

"Excuse me," a man said as he approached. "I'm sorry to interrupt. You've been invited to dine with the warriors this evening," he said to Scarlett.

"Oh. Okay," Scarlett said. She turned back to the scout who obediently started to climb out of the bed.

"Wait!" Scarlett said. The scout froze. "You should probably stay here and rest."

"Yes, master," the scout said, settling back into bed.

"Scarlett," Scarlett corrected her.

"Yes, Scarlett."

Scarlett paused, about to say something else, but then changed her mind. She shook her head. *What did I just get myself into?* she wondered as she turned to follow the Eagle out of the room towards the dining hall.

47

THE DINING HALL was a cacophony of raucous, victorious voices and clattering silverware. When Scarlett entered, the voices hushed and they all stared at her. Scarlett stood there awkwardly, unsure of what to do.

"Uh . . . thanks for letting me eat with you," she said.

They stared at her.

"Okay, stop staring, this is weird," Scarlett said.

The Eagles slowly returned their attention to their plates and their murmured conversations began again, slowly picking up steam until the room had returned to its previous din. The Eagle who had escorted Scarlett to the dining hall directed her towards a buffet line where food was piled high on massive platters, despite the fact that most of the plates in the room looked to be full. Scarlett walked over and loaded her plate with meat and tortillas and beans and rice and vegetables until the plate was nearly as heavy as the scout had been when Scarlett had hauled her out of the Slaver compound.

Remember, you have to eat slowly she silently instructed herself. *The only thing you've eaten in the last week is a couple cans of beans. If you eat too much too fast, you will throw up. Nobody wants to watch you throw up, even if you are a legendary warrior.*

Scarlett scanned the room, looking for an empty seat, but the room was practically packed from wall to wall. Then, she saw a face she recognized and crossed to the far end of the hall.

"Mind if I join you?" Scarlett asked.

Néron looked up and smiled.

"Sure," he said, scooting over on the bench to make room for her. Scarlett sat down and took a bite of her food, relishing the taste of the spiced meat as it caressed her tongue. Holy shit, had she missed eating food. Scarlett quickly became aware that the other Eagles at the table were staring at her.

"Hi," she said, swallowing her mouthful of food. "I'm Scarlett."

The others murmured hellos and slowly returned to their own meals.

"Why does everyone here have a staring problem?" Scarlett whispered to Néron.

"You killed the Slaver Grand Master with your bare hands. The other people in the compound heard the story, but the people in here actually saw you on the battlefield," Néron explained.

"Ah," said Scarlett, taking another bite of food. The tomato was rich and tart and it took all of Scarlett's restraint not to let her eyes roll back in ecstasy. "So what happened after I passed out?"

"You mean after you used that foul language and passed out?" Néron asked.

"Hey, I said I'd stop swearing if I couldn't handle all those Slavers," Scarlett said. "I think I've earned the right to a few curse words."

Néron considered this and nodded.

"But only a few," he capitulated. Scarlett laughed.

"Anyway, what happened?" she asked.

"Well, with the Grand Master dead, the remaining Slavers fled. We were able to take the compound and claim it for the Eagles."

"Congratulations," Scarlett said. "That's what you wanted, right?"

Néron nodded.

"It's the first step, anyway," he said. "When the battle was over, we brought you back here." Néron took a bite of his food and Scarlett nodded.

"Hey, what happened to that one woman? The one that was all upset about the cream?" Scarlett asked, glancing around. "She's not going to leap out from behind a table and stab me, is she?"

Néron shook his head, the smile disappearing from his face.

"No," he said. "Brenna is . . . well, I can't really say where she is right now." Néron sighed heavily, the weight of this story evident on his face. "She dishonored the Eagles by putting a personal vendetta ahead of the tribe's goals in battle. Even worse, she did so at the expense of Eagle lives."

"You guys are big on honor, aren't you?" Scarlett asked.

"It's our most important virtue," Néron said seriously. "We value honor and warriors, and to dishonor the tribe, especially as a captain in our military . . . it's unforgivable."

Scarlett nodded.

"What will happen to her?" Scarlett asked.

"She will be exiled," Néron said. "This would normally be punishable by death, but her former rank as a captain affords her the privilege of keeping her life." He considered this. "Then again, the desert isn't kind to those that travel it alone."

"Yeah, I know," Scarlett said.

"How did you do it?" Néron asked. "When we found you, you didn't even have shoes."

"Don't I fucking know it," Scarlett muttered. Néron glared at her. "Hey, you said I get a few!"

Néron grumbled, but didn't object.

"And honestly, I'm not sure how I did it," Scarlett continued. "I'm good at what I do, but left with nothing like that . . . I don't know. I just put one foot in front of the other, I guess."

"What do you do when you're not running naked around one of the most dangerous deserts in the region?" Néron asked.

"I'm a mercenary for hire."

"Alone?"

"No, I had a team," Scarlett said. "And a . . . and I had a partner." She really didn't want to talk about Mel just then. She'd have plenty of time to think about her later.

Néron studied Scarlett, but didn't press her.

"I hear you're taking the slave with you," Néron said, changing the subject.

"So it seems," Scarlett said drily. "Our paths are intertwined."

"Yes," Néron agreed. "They are." He sounded so sure of himself, just as the High Elder had, and Scarlett didn't bother to question it. Néron stood up and picked up his empty plate.

"If I don't see you before you leave," he said. "Good luck."

He held out his hand to Scarlett, who shook it.

"Thanks," she said. "I appreciate that."

Néron turned to walk away, but stopped and sat back down beside Scarlett. He set down his plate and took off the leather cord looped around his neck, the one attached to a single red feather, and handed it to her.

"If you ever need assistance from the Eagles, show them this," Néron said. "Even though you're not one of us, they'll honor what it means and give you whatever you need."

"And what does it mean?" Scarlett asked as he stood up.

"It means you're a foul-mouthed warrior who did us a favor," Néron said with a smile before he turned and walked away, dropping off his plate at the front of the hall before leaving the room. Scarlett looked down at the feather dangling at the end of the necklace and held it between the thumb and forefinger of her unbandaged hand.

"A fucking feather," she said affectionately.

48

THE NEXT MORNING, shortly after dawn, Scarlett and the scout stood at the edge of Eagles' Pass. They had each been given large packs filled with clothes, rations, and extra ammunition, as well as a rifle each. Scarlett had a hunting knife strapped to her belt as well, and, at her request, four extra pairs of socks in her pack. The scout, however, was still wearing her vest and loincloth from the Slavers.

"Where are we going?" the scout asked.

"Oh," said Scarlett. "I actually don't know."

Scarlett took off her pack and searched inside for a map. She finally located it in a waterproof side pocket and pulled it out, unfolding it on the ground in front of her. It was a map of the entire North American continent and Scarlett squinted her eyes, trying to locate their position on the map.

"Where is Eagles' Pass?" she finally asked.

The scout crouched down beside her, briefly studying the map.

"There," the scout said, pointing with her finger. Scarlett stared in disbelief. She looked a little lower on the map and saw the Coahuila Desert labeled clearly below Eagles' Pass.

"I'm in fucking *Mexico*?!" Scarlett shouted in disbelief.

"Didn't you know?" the scout asked.

"No!" Scarlett exclaimed. "The last place I was before I woke up naked in a desert was way the fuck over here!" she said, pointing over at Virginia.

"Oh," the scout said. "That's far."

"Yeah," Scarlett said. "It is."

Mel, you fucking whore Scarlett thought bitterly as she refolded the map and stuffed it back into its pocket.

"Is that where we're going?" the scout asked.

"Eventually," Scarlett said. "We'll need more supplies than this to make that kind of a journey."

The scout nodded as Scarlett picked up her pack.

"By the way," Scarlett said. "We're going to have to talk about your clothes."

"Why?" the scout asked.

"Because you can't just go running around practically naked," Scarlett said.

"Why not?" asked the scout. "You were naked until yesterday."

"Yes, but that wasn't by choice," Scarlett explained. "I also sustained extra injuries without clothes like cuts and bruises and foot injuries and sunburns. Clothing helps to avoid that."

"Oh," said the scout. "But I like my clothes. My masters gave them to me."

Scarlett sighed.

"But they're not your masters anymore," she explained patiently. "Don't you want to wear something else? Something you choose?"

"Will you choose for me?" asked the scout.

"No," said Scarlett. "I think it's important for you to choose for yourself." Scarlett watched as the scout's face fell. "But I could help you, I guess. While you're learning."

The scout's face lit up.

"Oh, good! Oh, I can't wait to see what you pick for me!" the scout exclaimed.

Scarlett sighed again and looked out at the road ahead. Underneath her shirt, she could feel Néron's red feather brushing against her skin.

"Well," said Scarlett. "We'd better get going."

The scout followed obediently and the two women fell in step with one another as a lemon sun rose high above their heads.

About the Authors

E.S. Fortune is the evil genius behind 1602 Enterprises. When he's not running an empire or concocting weird and wonderful stories, he enjoys spending time with his three kids in his home state of Texas.

Emily Regan received her M.A. in creative writing from Northern Arizona University and is the author of several books, including *The Cloud Chronicles* series and *What's an Adult? No One Knows Anything and We're All Going to Die*. She currently resides in northern Arizona with her husband, son, and two dogs who sit patiently at her feet while she writes (the dogs, not the husband and son).